Miracles Not Included

By

I0653011

C. A. King

Cover Design: Lia Rees at Free Your Words

Editor: J.D. Cunegan

This book is dedicated to Jimmy
Gone, but not forgotten

Look for other books by C.A. King, including:

The Portal Prophecies:
Book I - A Keeper's Destiny
Book II - A Halloween's Curse
Book III - Frost Bitten
Book IV - Sleeping Sands
Book V - Deadly Perceptions
Book VI - Finding Balance

Tomoiya's Story:

Book I: Escape to Darkness
Book II: Collecting Tears

Surviving the Sins:

Book I: Answering the Call
Book II: Pride

When Leaves Fall: A Different Point of View Story

Peach Coloured Daisies: A Cursed by the Gods Story

Flower Shields: A Four Horsemen Novel

Copyright © 2018 by C.A. King

Cover Design: **Lia Rees at Free Your Words**

First Printing: March 2018

ISBN: 978-1-988301-33-4

Kings Toe Publishing
kingstoepublishing@gmail.com
Burlington, Ontario. Canada

From the Author's Desk

A child sat on the floor with a shiny new toy. It was exactly what he wanted, yet it fell to the side, simply existing, but never properly used. It had the potential to be so much more than a missed opportunity. Someone didn't heed the warning label or perhaps couldn't be bothered to run out and find batteries. It would have been an entirely different scene if they had. Adventure, learning and fun were there for the taking.

In the story that follows, life was that toy and miracles, the batteries. As the title may have given away, they most definitely were not included. Above, the child simply found another toy to play with. People, however, have been given only one life - finding another was never an option. To make the most out of hers, the main character, Chris, needed to read the labels; to notice the signs; and, in the end, to find a way to bring her miracles home.

Like batteries, having one didn't ensure an unlimited lifetime of use. There were times when Chris found herself in need of more. It was a good thing the world was full of them. It was only a matter of knowing where to look. Once she found out, all that was left was to reach out and grab a hold.

In a society that loved all that glittered and shined, it was easy to forget that not all miracles were those requiring leaps of faith. Not everyone was able to bear witness to the parting of a sea or water turning to wine. Throughout history, smaller scale miracles happened all the time, lacking only the notoriety that accompanied their more elaborate counterparts. On a personal level, they occurred even more frequently. It was up to individuals to see them for what they were. If a lemon tree grew in someone's backyard, they needed to decide what to do with the lemons. It was their choice to make lemonade; to share with friends and family; or to do nothing, letting the fruit grow, fall and rot away. Utilizing a miracle given was the key to making the most out of life.

Chapter One

Jason inhaled. The smoke no longer caused discomfort and coughing as when he first started. Now, all he felt was a momentary relief from the stress that had forced him from his new office in the first place. It wouldn't last. Another deep breath gave him the confidence he needed to start the trek back. For now, the craving had subsided, waiting for the opportune time to reappear without notice - perhaps rearing its ugly head during a mid-morning coffee break or his routine after-work scotch.

He studied the remaining size of the butt held firmly between two fingers. There was one remaining drag. He inhaled the toxins before tossing what was left aside. Ashes scattered onto the pavement as it fell. An elderly woman shook her head, her disapproval carrying as little weight on his mind as had the powdery remnants of the stick he'd thrown away. A chuckle escaped his lips, tied tightly to the lingering silver-grey cloud.

A part of him expected to be hit by the woman's purse in the same way the cat was always beaten in cartoons by the sweet old grandmother. That poor cat was doomed to an eternity of punishment for following what came naturally... chasing a bird.

People were so quick to judge others. Most of them had no idea what he was going through. He'd grown up at the tail end of the cigarette boom. The warnings were starting to come out, but they had been so poorly handled that the ads actually had the opposite effect on many a rebellious teen. Smoking became more than just a social delight - it was a way to stick it to the Man. Who was the government to regulate the rights of any citizen, man or woman? Looking back now, he realized he had hardly been a grown man.

The corners of his lips curled up, remembering the local malls when they first announced they were going smokeless. It was nothing more than a game to see if one could make it from one set of doors to the other with a lit cigarette in hand. It didn't matter if they openly showed off their disregard for rules, or pulled the sleeve of a sweater down to try to hide it, making it to the other side was all that mattered. If anyone managed to beat the odds, they came out of it with a new appreciation for what chickens had been going through for years. There was no reason why they did it other than being able to.

The punishment for being caught was merely a slap on the hand and perhaps a temporary ban. The reward was well worth it in comparison. He'd received many a hero's welcome in the form of cheers waiting at the end. That short walk could make a legend out of a poor sap who previously had no friends, even if it was only for a short time. That was peer pressure at its finest - the glory days of the cigarette.

It wasn't long before things changed more drastically. Smoking sections appeared, being little more than small rooms filled with clouds of smoke that hung heavy in the air like a thick fog. Whoever thought they were a smart idea had a few rocks loose in the noggin. Walking into one of those rooms probably did more damage to lungs than smoking for a year or two, maybe even more. It was concentrated nicotine - a place where one didn't even need to smoke to end up with a head rush from satisfied cravings.

The firm he worked for held out until the very end. Even then, his boss continued to smoke behind closed doors. No one was going to tell him what he could or couldn't do in his own office - at least until enough complaints started coming in.

Things, of course, continued to change. There were new studies and new warnings. It became less about personal rights and more about the health of children. Who knew the government could actually be right about something? By the end of the era, a revolution was in full swing, bringing with it stiff penalties and fewer places that catered to smokers. Some managed to quit. For Jason, it was too late. He was hooked. That meant every day he braved a crowd of holier than thou gawkers, ready to condemn him as an evil overlord.

Jason mumbled a few choice words under his breath. Street vendors were the worst part of his walk. He'd already passed one flower cart and was approaching the second of the three that littered the sidewalk of an otherwise enjoyable park. He held his head down. Any eye contact could be construed as an invitation for a sales pitch. Once a passerby was hooked, a good fifteen to twenty minutes was easily wasted. He had no plans to buy flowers and no desire to be reminded that he didn't have anyone to buy them for. His pace quickened, hoping to hurry past unnoticed. Out of the corner of his eye, vibrant colours caught his attention and something else - an insect. He couldn't remember the last time he had seen one, especially not as beautiful as this one was.

The butterfly fluttered before him. Its blue and yellow paper-thin wings were reminiscent of falling petals. Origami perfectly crafted from tissue paper couldn't have opened and closed as delicately. His breathing ceased, frightened even the smallest movement would disturb the majestic creature before him - a being pure enough that it didn't judge him for his shortcomings. If he had the ability to freeze a moment in time, that would have been it. He didn't, though. With a twitch of its antennae, the butterfly danced on the wind across the park.

Jason's chest heaved up and down - following might not have been one of his better ideas. He propped himself against a tree, needing a moment to catch his breath. If the butterfly could rest, so could he, at least until he didn't look as if he had just run a marathon. It wasn't, by any means, a case of being overweight. Such a short brisk stroll should have been a... walk in the park. The cigarettes were to blame. That damn addiction was sure to one day be the end of him. He knew it, but it didn't matter. Smoking was as necessary as drinking water.

"Are you alright?"

"Fine," Jason answered, holding up one hand.

The butterfly landed on the back of a park bench. He'd been too busy in his own thoughts to notice the woman who had already been seated there. He gave her a once over, looking for whatever the butterfly had seen. There must have been something special that made his tiny new friend stop there. He came up blank. She wasn't glamourous or even fashionable. All he saw was a woman who was considerably younger than him. He conceded that she wasn't bad looking, but his exact opposite. Where he stood dressed in a perfectly pressed suit and well manicured, she had more of a thrown-together look with tied back dirty blonde hair and mismatched clothes.

A strand of hair fell loose to the side of her face. Long thin fingers pushed it back behind her ear. His mouth went dry, all of the moisture magically appearing on the palms of his hands. They weren't soaked, but damp enough it warranted wiping them off on a handkerchief. Perhaps it was true - opposites did attract. He wanted to chuckle, but it came out as more of a huff than anything else.

"You look as if you were in a hurry," she commented. "Are you sure you are okay?"

"No," he answered. "I was following that butterfly."

A glow accompanied the woman's reply smile, leaving his stomach in turmoil. There was something hypnotic about the way her hand moved furiously, the lead of a pencil leaving scribblings on white paper. All her attention was focused on the blue and yellow colours of her bench mate. Not once did she look down at her notes or over at him.

Every second he remained there, he risked being labelled a creepy stalker. Normal people didn't stand in a park staring at single women without being noticed. The only thing that could have possibly been worse was if he had lit a cigarette at the same time.

Wasn't this a conundrum? He simply couldn't pull his eyes from the exchange taking place between the woman and the butterfly. Perhaps in a past life the two had been friends. His lips curled up at the realization he'd just sounded like his late mother. It had been a while since he thought about either of his parents.

"Are you a writer?" he blurted out.

Her eyes shifted in his direction. "What was your first clue?"

"Right," he replied, pursing his lips together. "I won't bother you, then."

"Wait," she called to his back. "Why were you following the butterfly?"

Jason's hand rubbed the back of his neck as if forcing himself to turn to face her. "It's silly, really," he answered. Specks of gold in his eyes reflected the light of the sun, each starting their own dance as if a party had just begun.

"When I was younger," Jason began, "my mother told me a story. For a brief moment, that butterfly reminded me of it."

"I'd like to hear it," she said.

He took a deep breath. "She believed butterflies were the messengers of angels. If something was missing from a person's life; if one fell off their intended path, a butterfly would appear to give them direction."

"Do you believe that?" she asked.

"I'm not sure," he replied.

"I'm Chris," she said, extending her hand.

"Jason." He returned the gesture with a firm, but not overpowering shake.

"It's an interesting theory," she continued. "Are you going to following it all day?"

"That might be difficult," Jason replied, his eyes motioning to the empty spot on the bench. "I think this messenger has flown the coop."

The lines between her eyes furrowed in disappointment. "Now we'll never know where it was leading you. How sad."

"I think I already know," Jason answered. "It led me to you."

Chris giggled. "That's a possibility, I suppose."

"I know this is going to sound strange," Jason started, "but can I buy you dinner?"

Chris opened her mouth, but only an "I," came out.

"If you are worried about safety, we can meet at a restaurant of your choice," Jason offered. "As public or private as you like."

Chris side-eyed him from the bench. "You really want to take me for dinner?"

"Why not?" Jason asked.

"I wouldn't have thought I'd be your type," Chris answered.

The truth stung. His normal dates were sophisticated business women who, undoubtedly, had their lives and outfits coordinated for the next few decades. "Perhaps you aren't," Jason admitted. "But then I'm still single, so my usual type isn't doing much for me."

Chris laughed. "Alright," she agreed. "Tonight at the Italian restaurant across the street. Say seven o'clock?"

"I'll be there." Jason said, smiling. "Out of curiosity, what's your favourite flower?"

"You don't have to buy me flowers," Chris replied.

"Indulge me," Jason said. "For curiosity's sake. If you were to buy yourself flowers, what would be your choice?"

"You are seriously asking me about my opinions on flowers?" Chris replied, shaking her head. "Okay. On West Street, there are three flower carts. Do you know them?"

Jason chuckled. "Yes. I passed two of them today already."

"I'd pick a bouquet from the middle cart," Chris stated.

"Why the middle one?" Jason inquired.

"It's different," Chris answered, shrugging her shoulders. "The other two sell only roses. The one between them offers a variety."

"You don't like roses?"

"It's not that," Chris replied. "It's silly, really."

"How so?"

"Roses are beautiful flowers," Chris explained. "Everything about them draws you in from their delicate petals in pristine shades: red; white... black, to their subtle scents - enchanting perfume that teases one's senses. It covers just about everything: sight; touch; smell - all of it luring you into a false sense of security. Once it has your trust, it draws blood."

"Draws blood?" Jason ask.

"Thorns," Chris replied. "Roses are the vampires of the flower world."

Jason laughed - not a chuckle this time, a warm hearty laugh, the type people found contagious. "I don't know how you came up with that from looking at a rose, but... I like it. Tonight should be interesting."

"I hope so," Chris blurted out. "There aren't many people who can handle a night of possibilities."

"I have a feeling I'm the exception," Jason replied. "Possibilities might be just what I need a night of."

With a spring in his step and a whistle on his lips, he headed back to work. His hand dove into his pocket, returning with a silver coin. Using his thumb, he tossed it in the air, catching it on the way back down. It didn't matter what side it landed on, he was a winner. That was the day his luck changed. This woman was the cure for all that ailed him, body and soul.

Chapter Two

Five years later...

Morning. The best time of the day to be productive. Chris threw open the curtains, letting the warm rays of the sun meet her soft, freshly washed face. Eyes closed, she mentally recorded every moment, preserved for use in a book somewhere down the line. That was what being a writer meant. Every thought; smell; or feeling, broken down into words in her mind. She sighed, knowing the moment would be cut short.

Having the morning sun at her back as she wrote was a premise that worked better on paper. It had been pure heaven with a touch of romance when she described it in her third novel. In practice, however, it meant the curtains needed to be drawn or she wouldn't have been able to see the screen on her laptop properly.

The sun's story in all its glory would have to be silenced, at least for a little while or she would never complete her latest endeavour. A new genre was hard enough for her to break into without distractions and glares were the worst type of those. That was probably why most of her online author friends swore by writing in the middle of the night.

When she started her career years ago, Chris decided she was going to create something for everyone. Recently, she realized that included horror. A chuckle escaped on her breath. How ironic; the thought of writing frightening scenes was her worst nightmare. Luckily, inspiration was everywhere, even in the upscale, backyard-using neighbourhood they had bought a house in.

Jason wanted to live in one of the more prestigious areas. She wanted room to grow. As an only child, having a large family was on her to-do list - it just hadn't happened yet. That was why she agreed to move there. When it was time for the pitter-patter of tiny feet, they were already set in the perfect home.

Every street in the area was lined with large family houses complete with perfectly landscaped gardens and white front porches. Swings hung from overhangs on some and bistro seats or Adirondack chairs sat on others. It didn't matter what the furnishings were. That part was all for show. No one ever sat out front of their homes around there. Too much money had been spent making their backyards the envy of the rest of the town. There was no doubt they lived on a street of backyard retreats featuring swimming pools, trampolines, outdoor kitchens, and garden sheds turned into offices. If it could be done in a yard, someone around there probably had already done it.

She turned her attention to directly outside the bay window. The heavy material curtains flew closed. Chris crunched down, squatting. One eye strained to see through the remaining small slit to the world beyond.

"What are you doing?" Jason asked, leaning against a wall, coffee in hand. He ignored the steam, taking a mouthful and managing not to flinch at the burning sensation that reminded him of smoking. It eased the cravings enough in the morning until he could satisfy them fully.

"Sh," Chris whispered, waving one hand behind her back at him. "It's the neighbour. He's doing something strange out by the road."

"You don't think he can hear us, do you?" Jason said, chuckling. "We're inside. So what's he doing that has you all riled up? Let me guess, wrestling bears?"

"He's pouring something down the sewer drain - a reddish brown liquid. I think it could be blood. Is that coffee for me?"

Jason laughed. "Blood?" he quarried. "That's a little far-fetched, don't you think? It's daytime. I'd think if he murdered someone, he'd clean it up at night. With people heading to work and kids off to school, there are way too many witnesses."

"That's what he wants you to think," Chris explained. "You have to admit, it's rather odd to see anyone pour something down the street drain. Is that even legal in itself?"

"He's probably cleaning out his garage," Jason retorted, fetching a second cup of coffee. He added a little extra cream and a teaspoon more sugar, exactly the way his wife liked it. "It's on your desk."

"As I recall, you did that last week," Chris said, trying to ignore his offering. "You used a hose and washed the dirt down the driveway. I didn't see you use any containers or coolers to lug dirty water to the road." Her nostrils flared, inhaling the scent of the freshly brewed java. He'd placed it out of her reach on purpose, toying with her.

"I'll give you that," Jason replied. He gulped back the last of his drink. Placing the cup on the desk beside the other, he bent down to kiss his wife on the top of her head. "I'm sure there is a reasonable explanation. Would you like me to ask him on the way out?"

"No!" she exclaimed. "He'll know we're on to him. Don't tip our hand before the rest of the cards are dealt!"

Jason shook his head. "You're trying to write that horror novel again, aren't you?"

"What does that have to do with anything?" Chris complained. "How do you always know? It doesn't matter even if I am. This is weird behaviour."

"Your mind gets genre-focused," Jason stated. "Whatever you are writing becomes everything you see and do. Personally, I'd prefer you wrote a few more hot and steamy scenes." He chuckled at her attempt to swat him without taking her eyes off the unfolding scene outside.

"If you didn't like it," she argued, "you shouldn't have married an author." He'd known her personality from day one. She'd never hid anything from him and never would.

"I never said I didn't like it," Jason replied. "It's one of the things I love most about you - the way you see things no one else does. Nothing escapes your eye and you can read anything into even the simplest of events. My home life is an up close look into the mind of an author. How many guys can say that? Best part, I don't even have to read to get interesting stories. I just have to watch you."

"Your home life will be waiting for you when you come back," Chris said. "Your office life might not be so patient if you are late again."

"Right," Jason replied, grabbing his jacket off one of the maroon and beige high-backed chairs that complimented his wife's wooden desk. They were as much for show as the furniture that graced the front porches of the neighbourhood. An author's clients didn't attend an office to read. They perused pages in the comfort of their own homes, or perhaps a library. Still, Chris had wanted her writing space to have a sophisticated look and he'd caved. He always did. In a way, he was her own personal Santa, giving her just about anything she asked for.

"Don't make eye contact on the way out," she ordered before calling out, "I love you," just as the door slammed behind him.

He glanced back. The flashing around the door was starting to show signs of needing to be replaced. He added that to the growing list of household repairs waiting for him to the find time and energy to get to. Truth be told, he'd felt sluggish lately. That alone had already made him late for work a few times that month.

He flashed a smile at the neighbour, adding a friendly wave. A part of him hoped the man never found out the life Chris had invented for him.

Chapter Three

Fingertips blindly stretched to capacity, barely making contact with the notebook. Pencils scattered on the floor along with it. Chris flipped it open, paying no attention to the cute dogs begging for attention on the front cover. There was a time in her life when the designs were more important - chosen carefully for their appearance. Now, a journal was no more than a means to an end. Numerous scratch pads were scattered around her home for when inspiration hit, as well as two in her purse and several in both the cars. Days of using a napkin if nothing else was available were long gone. She was in an entirely new phase of her career. As for technology, it wasn't all it was cracked up to be. She'd just smile and make up an excuse when someone asked her why she wasn't toting around a laptop or tablet to write everywhere she went. Of course, the truth was being an author had been over-glorified, like every other profession.

Writing in a local cafe had a fun ring to it. She'd tried it a few times in the past. Between the distractions of life and people asking her questions every minute, she only managed to write one line and wasted several perfectly good evenings. Having a coffee and people watching would have been a better use of her time. At least that was research.

Then there were the outlandish ideas that she could somehow don a bikini with a large floppy hat and sunglasses; lie on a lounge chair by a pool on a hot summer day; and put the laptop on her legs to create a romantic masterpiece. If anyone actually took time and thought about that scenario, they'd have realized it could never happen. First, bright sun and sunglasses were both counterproductive to seeing a screen and second, laptops, heck even phones, tended to overheat in direct sunlight and hot temperatures. That didn't even take into account what would happen if a splash of pool water made contact with one of them. She'd lose a whole day while her computer took a rice bath, and even then, there were no guarantees it would ever work again.

The tip of her pencil snapped. She tossed it over a shoulder and felt around the carpet for another one. As long as the neighbour's suspicious behaviour was in full view, she was going to take advantage of the situation. The new pencil began its work, scratching out barely legible words and random thoughts. It wasn't only what he was doing, but how he looked doing it. The man wasn't hard on the eyes, which made it even easier to keep watching.

It had nothing to do with her husband. Jason was, by all means, a perfect man. That sophisticated magazine hunk style - from his three-piece suits to his perfectly fashioned hair, including a well-kept beard and moustache was what made her agree to go out with him in the first place. Her fingers traced her lips, remembering the feeling of their first kiss. The neighbour, however, had more rugged good looks, right down to the toned muscles that flexed when he lifted a container of liquid to empty. Those muscles! The skin-tight shirt he was wearing left little for her imagination to do.

A groan couldn't be contained, making an escape from her slightly parted lips. How could she not find him attractive? The way he stood up straight and used the back of his hand to brush the sweat from his brow was movie worthy. It was the perfect scene - if she could capture his movements in words, she'd have the makings of a bestseller in any genre. He was definitely main character material, well at least his appearance was. She'd make his character fit the plot. That was, after all, her job.

Chris returned to making notes on what the liquid could be. Blood was the obvious first thought. But why? That question was hard to answer when she knew so little about him. He'd moved in a few months back, if her memory served her correct, which it usually did. At the time there had also been a woman - short with long black hair. She had been stylish, but her fashion sense screamed office worker, not boss. It had been weeks since Chris last saw her.

It was possible the missing woman was a victim - dismembered in the garage after a random meet-up off some sleazy dating site gone wrong. Her mind began filling in details. The two would have met a few times before he brought her back to his lair, lulling her into a sense of safety... then bam, taking her out with a kitchen knife. Maybe she was tied up for days in a bedroom - tortured by those very muscles she had just been admiring. Her eyes widened, visualizing the unfolding story.

Her lips pursed together. It wasn't right. Scenes of torture and rape were hard sells and needed trigger warnings. That wasn't the direction she wanted to go with her writing. The murder part still could have panned out with some work.

Of course, she also could have been way off-base. A new conspiracy theory formed in her mind. One in which her neighbour was, in fact, a terrorist adding some strange bio-chemical mixture into the sewers - a man for hire, willing to do anything to stick it to today's society. There was always a message in those plot lines - a warning that the mainstream population needed to take notice of, but seldom did. That was a little too deep for what she was trying to accomplish. She wanted a horror story, not a thousand-page thriller with espionage.

The deranged lunatic idea also held possibilities. He could have been releasing baby alligators into the sewers beneath their quiet town - a maniac wanting to breathe life into old urban legends. If the liquid she saw had been reddened by a radioactive ooze, that could have been used to make them grow faster. Technically, goop like that was green in stories, but there was no reason why it couldn't be red. A group of hungry alligators living in storm sewers made the beginnings of a scary plot.

The phone rang. Her arm outstretched behind her, knocking it off the desk. "Hello."

"Hi," Jason said. "I wanted to remind you we have reservations for an early dinner."

"You just left," Chris cackled.

"Babe," Jason replied, "that was hours ago."

"Hm. I guess that means the coffee went cold..."

Chapter Four

Jason hung up the phone. The smile left over from his wife's words morphed into a blank stare. The car radio came on just long enough for the windows to go down. Years ago, he'd vowed to his bride on their wedding day they would quit smoking together. She'd found it easy. He'd struggled from day one, ultimately falling back into the dependency he'd found too hard to break free from many times before.

Secrets weren't something he wanted in their relationship, but here he was and the only thing he'd managed to give up were the walks in the park. The underground parking lot was now the preferred location for his quick fix. With nobody around, no one was the wiser. He worked hard to keep it that way. It felt dirty. It felt wrong. He was hiding like a junkie with a drug habit. What caused cigarettes to be considered that bad?

His hand reached under his seat and pulled out a silver container, his initials etched into the metal. His fingers traced the elegant lettering. He'd never been able to figure out what font had been used, not that it mattered. The flip top opened, revealing his darkest secret. Fire from the matching lighter flickered as it moved towards the end of the cigarette, hanging out of one corner of his mouth. The first inhale was always the best. He closed his eyes, enjoying the lightheadedness that spelled out satisfaction. Even the scent of his own exhaled smoke was a reward.

He flicked the ashes out the window, making sure to leave no visible trace before drawing in another breath to his lungs' capacity. This time, he watched the red embers at the end morph into grey ash. Ashes to ashes at his funeral was going to be an appropriate line. He laughed at his own morbid thoughts. It wasn't like he was dying, and even if he was, how much time would really be added to his life span if he gave it up now? It would have resulted in a few days at most. Was it worth the suffering for such a small fraction of life?

There would be time for guilt later, now it was time to relax. Tomorrow was a better day to quit. That five-minute break meant the difference between nailing his presentation that afternoon and a long line up at the unemployment office. The pressure was on - at least that was what he told himself. An addict always had an excuse and tomorrow wasn't ever going to come.

He examined what was left of the burning stick and took one last inhale before snuffing it out on the cement floor beside his black Mercedes. It was clean up time. The extinguished butt fell into a small sandwich bag. A bottle of fabric freshener spritzed the car, his clothes and hair. A touch of cologne and a couple of mints were the final touches. With the baggie in the trash, he took the elevator up to his seventh floor office, making a pit stop on the way.

Warm water and soap washed away any traces of nicotine stains on his fingers - a putrid yellow colour that he couldn't bear to look at. He glanced up at his own reflection, not recognizing the man staring back. He felt all washed up and looked it too. Maybe he was a junkie in that respect. Ever since his birthday, he'd been feeling as if he were falling apart. Was forty the magical age when the things done in youth began to catch up? There were aches and pains that joined a lethargic foreboding feeling on an almost daily basis together with a new respect for those who lived to see their senior years.

Glancing at his watch, he realized there wasn't time for the self-pity party. He splashed cold water on his face, dabbed it dry with a paper towel and headed back to work.

A few extra vitamin C tablets and some cold prevention medication was all any doctor would order. Why waste time seeing one? A chuckle escaped from the back of his throat. He figured a midlife crisis was a sports car and younger woman, not feeling sluggish. Then again, he already had a wife eight years his junior. Any younger and he probably wouldn't be able to keep up. She was a handful as it was, even if he did love her for being that way.

He freed his mind to concentrate on the biggest deal of his career. If he pulled off a win for the firm, he could afford to take a week or two off and catch up on some rest. A vacation some place warm was already going to be on the table for discussion at dinner, reservations for which were put in place months ago. Chris deserved a nice getaway. She was as much responsible for his success as he was.

When he'd met her he'd been a middle-of-the-pack advertiser. He knew all the right protocols and did his work efficiently, but, as his employer had always been keen on pointing out, the ads he created lacked a certain spark. Chris had a way of making him see the possibilities. It was that awoken imagination together with his learned skills that put him where he now was. She was the spark he'd been missing. Having found it, he never planned to let it or her go.

He may have failed at keeping one vow on is wedding day, but that was the only one he was going to break. To love, honour and cherish until death do they part weren't negotiable. He'd fulfill each one until he was in the grave, and maybe even after that.

Chapter Five

Chris couldn't believe she'd almost forgot it was Thursday, her favourite day of the week. It was date night. Jason had insisted on making it part of their wedding vows - the ones made to each other in private after the ceremony. They were both bound to forever more taking one night a week to go out for dinner. It was an opportunity to discuss anything in their relationship that needed discussing. Normally, that amounted to little more than upgrading to new appliances or vehicle leases.

There was no denying Jason's plan had worked like a charm for them so far. When accompanied with a bottle of fine wine and a delicious meal. it resulted in a happy marriage, exactly as he said it would. They had an honest and open partnership with no secrets and no real problems in their lives. For her, there was only one thing missing. One thing that could have made everything, as good as it was, better and she was going to make it the focus of the evening's discussion.

She glanced at the valet and then at the state of her car. He'd need an extra big tip. Empty wrappers and coffee cups lined the passenger side floor. Littering inside her own vehicle was a better choice than the ground. If the option had been available, she would have gladly parked and walked the extra hundred paces so no one had to see the mess. The attendant sped off, leaving her standing outside the five-star restaurant door in her little black dress. It was her go-to outfit for almost every occasion that required more consideration than usual. In this case, it probably wasn't enough.

Jason had mentioned dressing up, but failed to reveal it was a formal evening. If she had known, she would have at least put on some bling to distract from her lack of fashion sense. Jewelry she had plenty of. Other women would have committed murder to have a husband eager to toss shiny baubles their way... Chris, not so much. She was the person for whom the term low-maintenance was created.

When she left the house, her wedding rings always accompanied her - front and centre, ready to be seen by all. Earrings were okay... on special occasions. The rest was simply annoying. Necklaces or anything around her neck made her feel like she was choking. Bracelets got in the way of writing.

She shrugged her shoulders, held her breath and strutted through the door. No matter what she wore, she'd always been one to own it. That night wasn't going to be any different. What her outfit lacked in finesse, she made up for in attitude.

A new restaurant every week was part of the plan and in the past five years they'd manage to not repeat a single place, at least for date night. It was rare, however, for Jason to pick an expensive restaurant without prior discussion. He had to have known about this for some time. This wasn't a call on a whim eatery. It was a place where it took weeks in advance to book a table - the sort of posh establishment people came to get engaged or to break up without a having to worry about their partner making a scene.

From the entrance she had a partial view of busy tables filled with couples and families celebrating one occasion or another. An elderly couple sat side by side, years gone by reflected in their eyes. A group of women in their late twenties clanged glasses together before falling back into their chairs with a round of giggles to celebrate a looming wedding.

"Darling," Jason called out.

A polite smile graced her lips for the waiter she almost had to speak to. Chris was a writer. One might think that made words come easy, but that was only on paper. Dealing with people and crowds wasn't her strong suit. Luckily, it was Jason's. When they went out together, he handled the socializing. Outside of that, she had a handful of close friends: a select group from her teen years; a few fellow authors she had become well acquainted with; and her ever present social media besties.

The latter were the ones she chatted to on a daily basis and shared all her life's ups and downs with. They were there to like, cry, and support - whatever the case might require. Everyone needed validation from time to time and, in the age of technology, there was nowhere better to get it than the internet.

Jason held the chair for her, pushing it in as she sat - a true gentleman through and through. "I trust I didn't pry you away from your spy work."

"I prefer the term research," she replied. "This is a rather fancy choice for dinner." She eyed his movements, looking for any secrets they might reveal.

Jason poured red wine into her glass. "We're celebrating. I closed the deal today... the biggest the firm has ever handled."

"Tell me everything," Chris gushed, her eyes dancing with enthusiasm. Success was a much better reason for the expensive restaurant than avoiding an emotional break-up.

"There isn't much to tell," Jason admitted. "They loved my pitch and don't want to change a thing. That means I am entitled to some time off."

"Time off?" Chris echoed, wine glossing her lips with a shine.

"I know I've been a bit preoccupied and stressed out lately," Jason explained. "So... I asked for a couple weeks off. We can plan to go somewhere if you'd like."

"You know I'd be happy anywhere as long as we are together," Chris answered. They hadn't been away together since their honeymoon. A tropical destination held interesting possibilities.

Chris glanced over the menu, setting it aside immediately. It was in French - a language she knew only about twenty words in. The last time she'd been stubborn and tried to order for herself in that language, she'd thought she had requested roast beef and potatoes. Jason had teased her for weeks and even after that never let her forget the moment when the waiter brought out apples in a puff pastry as her main course instead.

She bit her bottom lip, listening to her husband order. There was no sense asking what it was. If she couldn't recognize it, she probably didn't want to know. It was the thought of eating some things turned her stomach, not the taste.

A basket of fresh warm bread wrapped in white linen made it to the table first. It smelled rich, promising mouth-watering goodness in every morsel. Creamy butter made the perfect topping. Her stomach approved with a growl before even a taste could be had.

"You skipped eating again today," Jason commented, lathering his own piece of bread. 'Maybe you should take a step back and not be so work obsessed all the time. I think a vacation will do us both good."

Chris nodded, her mouth too full to attempt speaking. Her eyes followed the basket as the waiter removed it from their table, left over bread still inside. A salad of mixed greens soon followed - the dressing undetermined. The bitter aftertaste could have been ignored if it weren't for the fact that the bread had been so perfectly delicious.

The wafting aroma of the main course held promise. She examined it carefully. It looked like chicken smothered in a dense white gravy. The first forkful passed through her lips. It tasted like chicken. That was good enough. As far as she was concerned, it was chicken. If she didn't ask, Jason wouldn't tell her otherwise.

She listened attentively to the details of Jason's day and places he'd considered as possible destinations, biding her time until the final course, dessert. She'd waited the whole evening to bring up her own topic for discussion. Now was her moment.

"There is something else I'd like to talk about," Chris said, following the statement with a mouthful of white chocolate cake. She dabbed the corner of her lips, knowing a bit had escaped. It was impossible to make it through a meal anywhere without something missing the mark. Tonight, she'd impressed even herself. Not a single thing had fallen on her clothing - a small success worth noting.

"Go ahead, my dear," Jason replied, the refined tone of his voice matching the ambiance of the rest of the surroundings.

"I want to have a baby," Chris announced.

"We already discussed this last year when we agreed to stop using birth control." Jason whispered. He eyed the room looking for eavesdroppers and gossipers.

"That's my point," Chris answered, wringing her napkin. "It's been a year. I think we may need some help. I'd like to look into a few fertility clinics."

Jason's fork clanged on his plate. His eyes slowly moved to match her gaze. A silence divided them like she had never felt before. In an instant, she wished she could take back the words she had uttered. Had she insulted his manhood?

A huff escaped his slightly parted lips. Using a pristine white napkin, he wiped the look of astonishment from his face, replacing it with a poor attempt at a smile.

"You know I'm not a religious man," he started, "but I do believe there is a greater power out there - one that has a plan for us; guides us; and knows what's best for us. I've always said part of what is wrong with our world today is the tidal wave of scientists thinking they know better than the divine forces." He held up a hand. "I'm not talking about medicine so much as other things. Fertility clinics are one of them. Babies are being born that were never meant to exist. If we are meant to have a child, it will happen. If it doesn't, maybe it's for the best."

"How could it be for the best?" Chris complained, her voice raising a little too high.

"That's not what I meant," Jason whispered, motioning for her to settle down. "I just think maybe there is a reason we don't know about now, but down the line would make us think twice about having a child."

"What reason could there ever be to not want a baby with the man I love?" Chris argued, tears forming in the corners of her eyes, threatening to unleash a tidal wave onto her half-eaten cake.

"How about a compromise?" Jason offered. "We try for a year and, if we still aren't pregnant, we'll discuss fertility procedures. Fair?"

Chris nodded, wiping a single tear from her face and sniffling back the ones not yet fallen. "Fair," she agreed.

Jason motioned for the bill - the rest of their dessert destined to remain uneaten. There was an unspoken line of etiquette. She hadn't just teetered on that line, she had jumped right over and waved hi for all the world to see.

It wasn't the people around them that bothered her. It was the look in her husband's eyes. She hadn't seen anything even remotely similar staring back at her before. Sadness; disappointment, tiredness - she couldn't decide which it was. Being able to see the possibilities in every scenario was a gift or curse depending on how one looked at it. At that moment, she had no idea what to think. For the first time in her life, she came up with a blank.

He kissed her on the forehead as they waited for the valet attendant to fetch their cars. She glanced up at him. A warm glimmer of love had replaced the previous foreboding she'd thought she'd seen.

"I'll meet you at home," he said.

She watched his car pull away as hers arrived. The lighting in the restaurant had to be to blame. It played tricks on her eyes. If it was anything more, she would have known.

Chapter Six

The only problem with the current arrangement for date night was leaving in separate cars. To save time, Jason came directly from work. While Chris didn't mind meeting him, driving home alone in the dark aggravated her anxiety. Scheduling an early sitting was better than having to breathe into a paper bag or take a little white pill, both of which were sure to make her brain a bit loopy.

It was early evening. Although the sun had begun its descent, there would be plenty of time before it disappeared. Chris glanced up at the street lights, beginning to buzz, signalling the start of their shift. They had one job: keeping the roads safe throughout the night. Each vibrated slightly, lights flickering on, one after the other, as if plotting a course for her to follow. The back roads were the best way to avoid the hustle and bustle of workers heading home to their families. Anything was better than sitting in traffic.

Wind whistled through her hair, the window fully open. Using air conditioning on a beautiful evening was a waste when nature offered so much more. She turned the volume up on the radio, belting out the words along with the song playing. The best part about living in a semi-rural neighbourhood was the country roads. It was true they weren't maintained as well as the more frequently used streets, but no one was around to hear her sing off key either.

A white van in front of her, the only other vehicle on the road, set the pace for the trip. Chris cringed every time she slammed on the brakes only to speed up again. The drastic changes in pace stirred her author's imagination. Even with a squint, she couldn't make out any of the numbers or letters on the licence plate. They were either rusted beyond recognition or covered up so as not to be read. Either meant trouble: robbers planning a heist; a robbery in process; a kidnapping; or even hit men. Her lips twitched from side to side. Hit men weren't likely - they would have made a better choice in vehicle. A vision of her neighbour disposing of body parts flashed before her eyes.

The van slowed again. The passenger tossed something out. Chris's car swerved, barely missing a garbage bag as it hit the pavement and rolled into a ditch at the side of the road. Tires squealed. Her car skidded, upset at being forced to come to a quick stop on the gravel shoulder. Another few inches over and she would have joined whatever it was that had been discarded.

Chris's lips quivered, her mouth hanging open. The realization that she'd witnessed a crime came as a shock. She wrote about them, but never actually lived them. Even worse, exactly how big of an offense it was had yet to be seen. Still shaking, she reversed to where she had a view of the bag glistening in the twilight. Her heart pounded. She'd played out similar scenarios in her mind many a time, but this wasn't one of her made-up plots. There was a possibility there was a dead body hacked into parts in that bag. There was also a chance it was plain old garbage too. She let out a squeal, frustration setting in. Why would anyone have the need to dispose of garbage like that?

She closed her eyes, pinching the bridge of her nose. She needed to stay calm. Options were limited. If she called the police and waited for them to arrive, she ran the risk of the killers returning to the scene, having noticed her at the last minute. Deranged lunatics could have been arguing at that exact moment over what nasty end to bring to the only witness' life. She could have also left and called from home - if curiosity allowed. A sigh battled for freedom, trying to escape her lips which had managed to pull themselves back together. She glanced over at the bag then back at the empty road. Light was fading fast. Fingertips tapped on the dashboard, trying to speed up the decision.

A small blue and yellow object landed on the windshield. At first, Chris thought it might have been a piece of paper, perhaps a clue to the crime. It wasn't. When she stepped outside, she realized it was what she least expected to see - a butterfly. It was rather late in the evening see one flying about. Their freedom started at dawn and ended at dusk. The time after the sun went down belonged to their evil counterpart - the moth. So little was really known about the world these insects lived in, at least in her opinion. She'd been toying with a story idea for years about the two actually being one and the same. She surmised the colour from the butterfly drained away with the sun, leaving plain colours behind at night. It was a two sides of the same coin tale.

"I know you," she whispered. "I saw you once before - the day I met Jason. What are you doing here, little friend? Shouldn't you be preparing for a good night's slumber?"

The butterfly's tiny legs moved back and forth, wings opening and closing as if clapping for her words. It took flight, circling her head twice before moving towards the ditch and landing on the black plastic bag.

"So you want me to open it too?" Chris asked.

All apprehension vanished - fanned away by tiny wings. She slid down the gravel bank, her feet sideways, coming to a stop at the bottom. Weeds, swayed in a light breeze, bending down as if pointing to whatever was hidden within the discarded bag. Nature was practically begging her to look inside.

She surveyed her surroundings. The road remained deserted. Crouching down, one hand pulled at the plastic, ripping a hole. A whimper escaped from within. Chris gasped, shredding the bag faster. There was something alive inside. Nothing else mattered - not the van; not the would-be killers; not the fading sunlight; not even the disappearance of the butterfly.

Chapter Seven

Chris's teeth clenched together as the front door creaked open. It still hadn't been fixed, but under the circumstances, she wasn't about to bring that up now. She tip-toed inside. There wasn't even a good reason for her quietness. Her whereabouts had to be explained in full and right away. She slipped her shoes off. Something other than her tardiness wasn't right. Jason wasn't tapping his foot waiting for her to walk in. The light in the entrance way brightened with a turn of the dimmer.

"Honey," Chris called out. The lines between her brows deepened. She called them her worry warts, not that they were warts. They were signs of troubled times - remembering every difficult moment for her.

Flashes of her childhood flooded her mind as she peered round each corner looking for an ambush much as she had for many years on Christmas Eve while waiting for Santa and unable to sleep. A new thought crossed her mind. What if she was too late? What if her neighbour had been there? The front door being in the state it was, it could have easily been pried opened. For that matter, Jason might have left it unlocked thinking his darling wife was only steps behind. She quickened her pace between rooms, worrying more about what she would find with every step.

Clearing the main level left a choice, up or down. Upstairs led to only bedrooms and bathrooms. Downstairs was what Jason called the living area. Chris referred to it as a man cave. Everything on the lower level was set up to satisfy the deepest desires of any inner child. The result - one large playroom filled with games, theater-style seats and the biggest television screen on the market. Her husband liked anything extravagant and he spared no expense showing it.

She pulled the handle and stuck her head inside the threshold. "Jason," she yelled down. There was no reply, but she could hear the chatter of the television. That was a good sign.

She glanced at the bundle still wedged under her arm and sighed. It had to stay on the main floor for now, at least until she had the chance to discuss the matter with Jason. She plopped it down and pulled the door behind her, not fully closing it.

Chris hung onto a side rail, descending slowly, still unsure of what was waiting at the bottom. Her heart quickened with every steep step down. Directly ahead lay the corner that, once turned, would verify or discredit the visions scrolling by in her mind.

Her breath released in one large huff. Not a thing appeared out of place. The brown leather chair was in a fully reclined position, the tips of Jason's feet visible. On the flat screen, a bunch of men played football - at least, what she thought was football. The only sports she knew anything about were the ones that characters in her books enjoyed. Actually having fun watching the few sporting events she'd attended with Jason was something she'd never admit to. It was strictly research and nothing more. So far, that had amounted to baseball, hockey and various Olympic sports, both winter and summer.

"Jason," she called. Her stocking-covered feet double timed after touching down on the plush carpeting. "Are you okay?"

Chris came to a full stop in front of the chair, hands on her hips, blocking any view her husband might have had of the game. Her arms fell to her sides, frown lines softening. She bent over, examining the man she had married as he lay peacefully unaware of her presence. The wife part of her urged her to shake him into existence - the writer insisted on memorizing every detail. The latter always won.

She was drawn to his hand still loosely attached to a crystal glass filled with whiskey sitting on the side table. From the looks of the melting ice cubes, it had been a while since he had last taken a sip and yet, even in his slumber, he hadn't fully given up on the idea of having another.

Putting her finger on exactly what was wrong with the picture was proving harder than even she could imagine. Lots of men fell asleep watching sports, even her best characters were known to do that from time to time. So why was seeing her husband do it so perturbing? Her fingers snapped. It wasn't odd that he was doing it, but rather it was odd she'd never seen him do it before. The only place she'd seen him sleep was in bed. He wasn't a chair drowser - not even in a car or on the train. That's what was strange.

She inched closer. His chest heaved up and down with the weight of every breath taken. That proved he was still alive and the glass did not contain poison as had previously crossed her mind. A little drool found its way out of the corner of his lips. Their pillow cases every morning were proof that wasn't unusual. He soaked one section every night, enough to warrant a daily wash.

As Chris straightened up, her lips curled down and the furrow lines returned. Had he always taken naps downstairs? She'd never considered that he came down there to sleep. Did she keep him up at night? She grasped her upper arms, covering her chest in the form of an X. Did she snore? She shook her head - that couldn't be it. He would have told her.

One finger extended, making contact with his shoulder. Her body jolted backwards, narrowly avoiding being swatted like a fly. She giggled at the loud snort that followed. She wasn't the one who had to worry about snoring. Sleeping while sitting up wasn't a good position for him.

"Jason," she called.

He barely moved.

Her frustration growing, she took in a deep breath and yelled his name.

"What?" His body jolted, the contents of his glass sent flying to the floor.

Chris cringed. They'd put in the carpet when they first bought the house and he'd managed to keep it spotless ever since. If he or any of his friends had spilled even a drop, it didn't show. She grabbed what was left of the ice cubes and returned them from whence they came.

"Are you tired?" Chris asked.

"Maybe a little," Jason replied, looking up at her from the spot of whiskey he was carefully daubing with a napkin.

"Do you sleep down here often?"

"No," Jason admitted. "How long was I asleep?"

"I don't know," Chris replied. "It's after ten."

"That late?"

"Yes," Chris affirmed. Given the circumstances, it wasn't the best time to bring up the bundle waiting upstairs. She turned to make a quick exit.

"So why do you still have your jacket on?" Jason asked, his hands rubbing against each other, satisfied the carpet was as clean as he was going to get it without professional help.

"Well," Chris started. Her mouth opened to speak, letting out a mix of garbled sentences and thoughts. She made a second attempt to string together a simple sentence, failing miserably. It was as if everything she was trying to express had collided together in her throat, bits and pieces becoming lodged.

"Breathe," Jason suggested. "Did something happen?"

She cringed at the sound of bumps behind her. Her head turned in time to see her bundle of joy skidding down the steps on its rear end, coming to a stop at the bottom. It tilted its head from side to side. Her face snapped back forward.

"What is that?" Jason asked, peering around his wife.

"A puppy," Chris replied, offering a full toothy grin. She bit down on her bottom lip, shifting her weight from one foot to another.

"I can see that," Jason said, rubbing the stubble forming on his chin. "Where did it come from? And why is it in our basement?"

"That's what I was trying to tell you," Chris explained. "Can I pour you another drink?" This conversation was alcohol worthy. The tiny dog circled her feet. She wobbled, almost tripping. "Miracle, NO!"

It was too late. She didn't have to look down to know what the tinkling noise meant. Her lips pursed together. Jason's carpet was having a bad night.

"I think I'll take that drink," Jason said, falling backwards into his chair.

Chapter Eight

"It's not that I don't want you to have a dog, Chris," Jason explained, pulling back the pure white silk sheets. He climbed in, folding them neatly over top of his body. "It's that I don't want to end up having to take care of him. I don't want to be that dog's owner. Do you understand?"

"You won't have to," Chris blurted out, jumping on her side of the bed, landing on her knees. Her wide eyes examined her husband for a soft spot.

"I have my hands full with you," he replied, sitting up far enough to kiss her on the cheek. He flopped back down, his head indenting a stack of firm pillows.

"He'd keep me busy," Chris explained. "Please."

"No," Jason answered.

"I'd take him for his walks myself," Chris said. "You've been telling me I should get more exercise. This is the perfect excuse. Please."

"I meant join a gym," Jason muttered back, rolling over so his back faced her. He reached across the night stand, turning off the lamp.

"He'd be perfect for research," Chris begged. "I've been wanting to write a character with a dog for some time. Please."

"Animals are not research," Jason grumbled. "They are living, breathing creatures that need a lot of grooming and attention. That's more than I have time for. And stop biting your nails. They look a mess when you do that."

Her hand came down hard on the mattress. He knew her too well. She sighed and rolled over. Jason rarely put his foot down, but when he said no, it meant no. Her Miracle would have to go... unless. A sly smile crept over her face. There was one ace left to play.

"Okay," Chris said. "I'll take him to the pound tomorrow."

"You'll see it's for the best," Jason mumbled, starting to drift asleep.

"I suppose," Chris said, emphasizing a sigh at the end. "I thought he might take my mind off having a baby." She peeked over her shoulder, looking for any signs of having struck a chord. "I know we said we'd try for a year before exploring fertility options, but..."

"It can stay," Jason said, rolling over into a sitting position. Slanted eyes shifted towards her. That was his weak spot. He hadn't been able to give her a family, yet.

"Thank you!" She hugged him before he could say another word.

"It's a trial basis only," Jason warned. "If things don't work out, it's straight to the pound. Keep it off the furniture and only on the main level."

"Deal," Chris said, her enthusiasm bubbling over into her smile. Her arms tossed around him, squeezing tight. A loud smack accompanied lips planted firmly on his cheek

"Great," Jason said. "Maybe now I can get some sleep. Tomorrow, take him to a veterinarian and have him checked out. He might have been hurt being tossed out of a moving car."

"I already did," she replied in her standard matter of a fact tone. "After I first found him. He had a bath too. I used the credit card... hope that is okay."

Jason groaned, pulling one of the covers over his head.

Chris fluffed her pillow and lay back. Her eyelids closed under the weight of the day's activities, her mind swirling with adventures. A low buzz interrupted what promised to be a pleasing dream to fall asleep to. Her eyes opened enough to survey the room. The noise ceased. She began her nightly ritual again. The dull sound returned.

"Jason," Chris whispered.

"Yeah," he replied.

"What's that noise?" she asked.

Silence filled the room. A low whining turned into a cry coming from the bottom of the stairs.

"That would be your dog," Jason replied, rolling onto his back again, eyes open. He sighed. It was a good thing he had that nap.

"Not that. I think Miracle is crying because of the noise." Chris complained. The buzz returned. "That! What's that noise?"

"I don't know," Jason admitting, throwing off the covers, His feet slid into soft slippers. "Why'd you call it Miracle?"

"It was a miracle he survived being thrown from a truck. It was a miracle I found him. It's definitely a miracle you let me keep him. It seems to fit," Chris explained.

"I'll tell you what a real miracle would be," Jason grumbled. "If I get any sleep tonight." He pulled on his robe.

"Where are you going?" Chris asked.

"To find out what that noise is," Jason answered. "And take your dog for a walk so we don't have a repeat of the mess that happened earlier."

"You think the noise is coming from the neighbour's house, don't you?" Chris asked.

"Don't give me that look," Jason replied. "I'm sure there is a reasonable explanation - one that doesn't involve murder."

"Still, be careful," Chris demanded. "I'm too young to be a widow."

"You look great in black," Jason jested. He rolled his eyes at her seriousness. "Don't worry, I will... and if I need to make a quick get-a-way, I'll sacrifice the dog."

Chris threw a pillow across the door, missing her mark and hitting the backside of the door as it closed.

Chapter Nine

Jason whistled. "Nice ride."

The neighbour's garage was split into two sections. The first was littered with wood, tools and paint cans. A thin layer of saw dust coated the cement floor, its granules shifting positions slightly in the night breeze. Hanging on the walls were power tools, most of which he had no clue what they were for. If that wasn't enough to turn his eyes green with envy, what was stored in the smaller section was.

In a spotless corner sat what amounted to every man's ideal toy. His imagination drifted, one leg tossing over the black seat. The key turned, engine purring as he caressed metal.

"I'm Jason." He extended his hand.

"Jon," the man replied, wiping his hands with a rag before accepting the greeting. "You ride?" He nodded towards his motorcycle.

"No," Jason admitted. "But I can appreciate the beauty of a well-oiled machine. It's as fine as looking at a beautiful woman. You had her long?"

"Long enough," Jon replied. "But she's not a midlife crisis, if that's what you mean. I have a number of years before I reach that. How about you?"

Jason chuckled, sly comment noted. "I married a younger woman," he said. "That took care of any crisis I might have had at the same time. I don't have to look for a model with less miles on it, if you know what I mean."

"Fair enough," Jon replied. "I hope I didn't wake you and your young wife."

"The wife," Jason admitted, his hand diving into his pocket. It returned with his tin and lighter. "Do you mind? Chris doesn't like me smoking so I try to keep her out of the loop."

"She probably knows more than you think," Jon suggested. "Those things leave a distinct smell that's hard to get rid of."

"Right," Jason said. He tapped the cigarette on the tin a few times and returned it without lighting a flame. "Before bed probably isn't the best time to try and hide it." His thumb turned the wedding ring on his finger.

Jon smiled, shaking his head. A piece of sand paper scratched across the surface of a wooden desk. Bits of paint disappeared, leaving behind a smooth surface where once had been a worn piece of furniture.

"So what are you doing here?" Jason asked. "Re-doing the house for the little lady? Getting ready for a new addition to the family perhaps?"

"I wish," Jon replied. "My wife is in the hospital. This is to pay the bills. Advanced cancer treatments are available for the right cost. We've already exhausted traditional methods. She hasn't given up the fight yet, so paying for it is the least I can do."

"Sorry," Jason offered, the ring spinning faster.

"It's not your fault," Jon replied adding, "directly," onto the end and nodding at his neighbour's pocket. "We live in a generation where everything causes cancer and not enough is being done to solve the problem."

"You'd think they'd have found a cure by now," Jason said.

"That's only part of it," Jon replied. "We know things that cause cancer, yet we still do them. I'm not just talking about cigarettes. There's a lot of other things too, even bacon. If society eliminated the causes, there wouldn't be a need for a solution. Of course, I don't expect to see anyone giving up driving and pesticides in the near future. There's too much money in it all; too many jobs to be lost. I also think the powers that be consider it a form of natural population control. There's no hurry to save lives when too many are being born every day. There's no room for the old anymore. Sacrificing a few of the young is a compromise I can see governments making."

"I never bought into any of the conspiracy theories before," Jason stated. "But you make a compelling argument. How long has she been sick?"

"We found out right after we moved in," Jon answered, eyeing the walls of the garage. "We bought this place thinking about a future - a family. We both always wanted a number of children... a big family."

"That could still happen," Jason offered, cringing at the thought of his own bride wanting a child for them via a fast track. "Cancer is nasty, but some people do get cured."

"We thought that at first too," Jon replied. "You put your faith into the system. You sort of have to, it's all you have. Then day after day, while you wait and watch, you can see the life leaving them - the patients, that is. Like a bright flame slowly being extinguished. Maybe God's pissing on it. All I know is one day it's gone and your loved one is lying there, nothing more than a shell, living for the sake of breathing and nothing more. You just know they will never be the person you used to know... to love." His voice faded off.

"That's brutal," Jason muttered.

"That's cancer," Jon replied. "It's too late at night for this depressing talk. Who's your little friend? He looks like he'd like to make it further than one house over."

"My wife's dog," Jason answered, looking down the tiny eyes hiding behind fluffed out fur. "She's supposed to be taking care of it entirely by herself." He rolled his eyes.

Miracle wasn't technically still a puppy, although his actions screamed otherwise. There had been no training classes in his past and it was obvious. Changing his ways now was going to take time and patience. There was plenty of pent-up love that needed to be set free. His tail wagged in a circle - a propeller preparing for take-off at a moment's notice. He tugged on the leash, his nose to the ground, sniffing out whatever he could find within his harness' perimeter. There were enough new scents to keep him occupied for now. If so much as a mouse appeared, even a full grown man would have a hard time containing his enthusiasm.

Jon laughed. "Then it makes perfect sense why you are walking him. How long have you had him? I haven't noticed any barking."

"She came home with him earlier tonight," Jason admitted. "I wasn't fond of the idea at first, but I think he might work out okay."

"Calling him *a he* is a good step," Jon said, smiling.

"What do you mean?"

"You called him *it* all night, but that last time you referred to the dog as *he*," Jon explained. "It's a good sign you are warming up to him."

"Maybe," Jason replied. "You never know, by next week I might even be using his name." He looked down and shook his head. "Nah." He turned back to the driveway. "We're off on an adventure," he joked.

"I'm packing up for the night," Jon called after him. "I won't be disturbing your young Mrs. anymore this evening."

"No worries," Jason said. "Maybe shut the garage door while using your power tools next time. I'll handle the little woman." He waved over his head as they headed down the sidewalk to finish their walk. He cleared his throat.

By the time he reached home again, he was out of breath and coughing. A late summer cold had knocked on his door. He'd been stupid enough to let it in. It was a good thing he had that time off.

Chapter Ten

"What happened last night?" Chris asked, almost climbing on his lap.

"I walked the dog and you fell asleep," Jason mumbled into his pillow, trying to shade his eyes from the light.

"What about the noise?"

"I'm trying to sleep," Jason complained. "Can I fill you in later?"

"Sure," Chris replied. "But it's four o'clock and you've already slept all day."

Jason threw the pillow off his head and turned to face the red lights displaying the time beside him. "I really slept that long?" he groaned, clearing his throat.

"Yeah," Chris replied. "I think you had a nightmare too." She pointed to his pyjama top. "You're soaked."

"I think I caught that bug that's going around," Jason said, using the back of his hand as a thermometer. "I feel a bit off... a scratchy throat and a bit of a fever."

"Well, go snooze downstairs," Chris ordered. "Sick or not, I need to clean the room and wash all the sheets. I'll bring you some soup." She held up her hand before he could move. "First, I want to know about last night. Did you find anything out?"

"You are relentless," Jason commented. "You know that, don't you?"

Chris simply smiled and nodded. She probably would have made a very good investigative reporter. All the skills were there and words flowed off her fingertips into paragraph form with only a little editing needed.

"His name is Jon and his wife is sick in the hospital," Jason confessed.

"Jon what?"

"What?" Jason asked.

"What's his last name?" Chris prodded.

"I don't know," Jason replied, pulling his legs around side of the bed. "I didn't ask him."

"Why not?"

"I didn't think it was relevant," Jason answered. "We're neighbours, not lifelong friends or business associates. He's the guy I wave to while cutting the lawn and say, "Hi, Jon.'"

"What's his wife's name?"

"What's with the drill?" Jason asked. "I didn't ask her name because I could tell he was in enough pain dealing with her being sick day after day. Before you ask, it's cancer and no he doesn't think she will ever fully recover."

"That's terrible," Chris mumbled.

"He's doing some handyman jobs on the side to pay for the medicines not covered by his plans," Jason explained. "That includes refinishing furniture. The stuff he was pouring down the drain was probably clean up from staining. I admit the sewer isn't the best place to dump it, but let's be honest, most of us clean up in a sink and that goes to the same place anyways. I think we should give the guy a break and some privacy. Promise me you'll leave him alone. He doesn't need to wind up reading about himself in a horror novel after living in the terror of dealing with his wife's mortality."

Chris simply blinked, not sure what to make of her husband's mood. He'd been cranky before, but today he seemed particularly perturbed about something. Maybe he'd seen more than he should have last night.

"Or maybe he's getting a cold," Jason said. "I know that look. There's nothing sinister going on next door. I'm going downstairs to watch television and rest. I trust you will let our neighbour have some peace and quiet too."

He stopped at the bottom of the stairs to glance down at the ragged ball of fur. "Have you walked him yet?" he called up.

Chris glanced down over the railing. "Yes," she answered. "We've been out four times today... once right before I woke you."

"Okay," Jason said, heading for the stairs down. He stopped for a moment and sighed. "Come on then. You might as well join me till dinner. I could use a miracle about now."

He smiled, watching the little dog scramble down the stairs, tumbling part of the way. A giggle tried to escape his throat, but came out as a mucusy cough. He grabbed a box of tissues before joining Miracle already curled up in a ball in his chair.

An hour was all Jason managed before waking to a deep husky cough. This one wasn't planning on leaving anytime soon. There was no way to disguise or muffle it. His face turned a shade of red mixed with purple - lacking the necessary flow of oxygen. Minutes passed with no signs of improvement. This wasn't an ordinary chest cold. There was no irritating tickle. It was as if he were choking - having the life sucked out of him by some unknown force.

Miracle's ears perked up, folding over at the top. A whimper of concern replaced playful barks and nips. He might have been new to the family, but they belonged to him now. A loud bark escaped his throat, summoning help.

"Are you okay?" Chris yelled, rushing to her husband's side. Her heart quickened at the sight of the man she loved slumped over on his knees. Her hand instinctively rubbed her husband's back.

Dread crept over her like the icy grip of the grim reaper. She could feel its touch on her skin, leaving a trail of goosebumps from top to bottom as a calling card. There was nothing she could do.

"Water!" She bolted for the tap behind the bar. A wine glass was the first to find its way into her grip; the tap already running; the water flowing out cool. She darted back, liquid splashing over the sides of the clear glass in her trembling hand. It sat on the coffee table, untouched.

Jason's shaking hands attempted to wipe the strings of saliva dripping from his lips in between gasps for air. The assault within his lungs continued. He grasped his sides, feeling each attempted breath as a kick in the ribs. He pressed tissues against his lips. One last intense hack left a bloodstained liquid on the soft white paper. The colour drained from his face. He'd been pale before, but this was a shade of white no person should ever become. A cold sweat formed on his brow. Either his eye sockets had sunken in or the rest of his face had puffed out. It was hard to tell which with the red circles that had darkened around them.

"I'm okay," Jason mumbled, gasping for air. He fell backwards to a sitting position on the floor.

"That's not okay," Chris replied. "I think you have more than just a cold. You need a doctor. This could be pneumonia."

Jason gazed down at the tissue's contents. "Yeah," he answered. "Can you call?"

"Forget calling," Chris replied. "We're going to the hospital."

Chapter Eleven

The automatic sliding glass doors opened and closed. Another batch of emergency care seekers rolled into the waiting room. Almost every seat was filled with one family tragedy or another. Children with fevers clung to their mothers, occasionally coughing up germs to share with anyone close by. A white towel covered one man's hand, the distinct red of blood starting to soak through its threads. The scent from an elderly gentleman who had managed to fall asleep indicated he probably should have been woken to use a restroom some time ago. They were stuck in a bodily fluid nightmare.

The nurse behind a sheet glass window called, "Next!" Her blank stare matched the plastic appearance of her face. She was a woman who had seen more than any one person should have in a lifetime and still had returned to see more. Sitting behind the protective shield, she seemed immune to the emotions that swirled around on the other side.

"Line ups," Jason complained. "You'd think they would see people in a reasonable amount of time." He stifled a cough, using his sleeve to block spreading more viruses than were already circulating in the air around them.

"They are overworked, underpaid and understaffed," Chris replied. "All things considered, it hasn't been that long." She unwrapped a cough candy and popped it between his lips, not caring if he wanted it or not.

"Four hours isn't that long?" Jason asked, rolling his eyes. "I've already waited here to see a doctor and waited to have the x-ray. Why do I have to wait for the doctor all over again?" He shifted in the plastic chair. The ones with even a little padding were claimed the moment anyone stood.

One television in a corner looped the news, volume on mute. Squinted eyes strained to read the captions flashing by, looking for distraction, but finding additional roots for depression. The dismal reports of the worst to happen in the world around them blended in perfectly with the solemn mood of patients. This place sucked hope out of people. It was a wonder anyone recovered from anything there.

"He is probably seeing someone else," Chris answered. "He can't very well leave in the middle of an examination because you are back. I don't like the hospital any more than you do." Each word stung, like a dagger plunging deep into her heart - the blade coated in a poison made from the memories of the loss of her parents years before.

"Whatever," Jason mumbled, rubbing his temples. A dull ache had formed, most likely from the pressure of the earlier attack. Every moment they waited, it gained strength and showed no signs of stopping anytime soon. His face scrunched into a frown at the increasing pain of the throbs. "Do you have anything for a migraine in there?" He pointed to her bag.

There were two types of purse carriers in the world. The ones who bought purses for fashion and those who needed something to carry everything and anything that might come in handy at some point. She fell into the latter category. Her hand disappeared, plunging in to begin its search. Having whatever was needed was never the problem. Finding it in the depths of a bottomless pit was a little harder.

"Jason Granet," a nurse called. She was as standard as any of the staff they'd met that night, cardboard cutouts, going through the motions without allowing an inkling of emotion show. Her job was to herd the cattle into the corral and nothing more. "Room four, down that corridor. The doctor will be with you soon."

"I've heard that before," Jason mumbled.

"Stop," Chris demanded, swatting his arm. She followed him into an examination room.

The scent of bleach burnt her nostrils, but was a welcome change from the previous seating arrangement. Their eyes took turns glancing at the watch on Jason's wrist.

A young man opened the door, flipping papers attached to a clipboard. "Jason Granet," he said without looking up. "I'm Doctor Antalen."

"Where's the other doctor?" Chris asked, giving up on the hunt for pain relievers.

"He's unavailable at the moment." The doctor's eyes shifted from side to side, immersed in the scribblings on the chart he carried. He sighed and put the papers down. "Are you a smoker, Mr. Granet?"

"He was," Chris answered. "He quit years ago."

The doctor shifted his gaze between husband and wife. "Is that true?"

Jason wasn't quick to answer. He found his head bobbing up and down in slow motion. "Pretty much," he replied.

"Pretty much," the doctor echoed, "or yes? It's one or the other. Either you quit or you didn't. There is no in between."

Jason ran his tongue over his bottom lip, leaving behind a thin layer of moisture. This was a trick question. He couldn't lie to a doctor, and at the same time, he also couldn't admit to his wife he had lied to her. His cheeks puffed out with air slowly escaping. The lesser evil needed to be the choice. "I have relapsed a few times over the years. A cigarette here or there on particularly stressful days."

Chris stared down at her hands, the ring on her finger prominently displayed. This wasn't the time or the place to discuss feelings of betrayal. Once Jason was better they could handle that issue. Her silence echoed loud enough to both men in the room.

"I'm not going to sugarcoat this," the doctor said. "The x-rays show a couple of spots on your lungs. I am referring you to the oncology department."

Chris's hand jerked to cover quivering lips. Oncology meant cancer - a deadly disease that few ever truly recovered from. Those that did were the exception, not the rule. Tears formed in the corners of her eyes, as if trying to dowse the burning sensation that had overtaken them. A battle ensued - one she lost as the first drop trickled down her cheek. Her head jerked to the side, hoping to hide her failure. Inside a nagging feeling took over - all that was good and right about her life was about to be plucked away. As hard as she tugged, she could already feel it slipping through her hands.

"You can head over there now and leave your information," the doctor said, adding new scratches of pen to the papers. "It's best to get on the list for the procedure as soon as possible."

"Does this mean I have cancer?" Jason asked.

"I can't answer that," the doctor admitted. "That's why you need to see a specialist. Even then, you won't find any answers until after a biopsy is performed."

"So there is a chance it could be something else?" Jason pried.

The doctor put the chart on his lap. "There's always a chance." He paused. "I'm going to prescribe you some liquid codeine to help suppress the cough so you can sleep. Take it only if you need it. Get that appointment booked as soon as possible."

"Thank you," Jason muttered, accepting the white note for the pharmacist. "Is there anything else I should do until my appointment?"

"Try to stay away from the internet. We see it far too often. Good folks like you drive themselves crazy with worry after looking up their symptoms. Do yourself a favour and wait for an official diagnosis. There is nothing you can do about the situation until then anyways."

"Thank you," Jason repeated, this time his voice weak and shaky.

The way home, silence was the disease they both fought and in the end lost to.

Chapter Twelve

Chris rushed to grab the phone after the first ring, not wanting to disturb Jason's sleep. After several nights of coughing, he'd finally given in. The codeine knocked him out within minutes and he'd been resting peacefully ever since. Between busying herself with chores and disinfecting every room, she found herself checking in on him. Her eyes searched for the up-and-down movement of his chest. Doubt had made a home within her soul and invited fear to come for a visit.

It had been two weeks since they registered at the oncology department of the hospital and his energy levels were at an all-time low. What had started out as silence between them had grown to a worry that ate away at their insides, slowly killing their strength. She'd tried to refrain from searching the web for information, but curiosity was the victor over reason. What she found was more than she bargained for. There were so many types and stages of cancer, it kept her mind running in circles. The worst part of Jason's case was where the disease was located - the lungs. There was no doubt that lung cancer was a killer, but if it was a different cancer showing up in his lungs, that was worse. That meant it had migrated from another location. It was literally travelling through the body and there was no way to pinpoint it or even track it. That type of cancer was inoperable and there was no cure.

"Hello," Chris said, moving her hair out of the way of the phone.

"Hello, is Jason Granet there? This is the oncology department calling."

"This is his wife," Chris answered. "He's sleeping. Can I take the information from you, or would you prefer I wake him?"

"That won't be necessary," the woman on the phone advised. "I am calling to let you know we've had a cancellation for tomorrow. Would your husband be able to make it?"

"Yes, of course," Chris answered, jotting down the information the woman on the other end was spewing out without pause. "Thank you," she said, ending the call.

Chris staggered into the sitting room, falling back onto the couch in an upright sitting position. Her legs may have turned to rubber, but her feet were solid concrete. She wasn't moving anytime soon. A finger caressed her bottom lip, begging for the uneven nail to be chomped on. There was no strength for biting, or moving. If breathing hadn't been a reflex, she probably wouldn't have been doing that either. She stared. Her gaze fixated on nothing and seeing exactly that. The burning sensation her eyes had become accustomed to in the past weeks returned. There weren't any eye drops strong enough to help.

The word *cancellation* echoed in her mind. No one gave up an appointment in the oncology department. They were simply too hard to come by. What that word actually meant was that a patient had passed away before receiving treatment. Someone had died to make room for her husband to have a slight chance at living. She'd never wished harm to anyone, but a part of her was thankful they had this opportunity. That part was glad someone else wasn't able to make it. Was she losing her humanity to selfishness? No one mattered more to her than Jason.

She felt her hand raise and fall. Chris sniffled, a weak smile crossing her face for a split second. "Miracle," she whispered. "How'd you know I needed a friend?"

A rough pink tongue lapped up the salty water covering her cheeks. She mused for a second at how dogs knew the exact way to make someone feel better in situations where people always failed. Then she remembered dogs couldn't talk, which meant they never said the wrong thing. Her hand caressed his fur. She buried her face in his side, instantly regretting it.

"You, my friend," she said, waving a hand in front of her nose, "need a bath. I can see I have been neglecting your needs. What do you say we go get soapy?"

Miracle barked, his rear end wagging along with his tail.

Chapter Thirteen

Chris pursed her lips together. There isn't much to do in a hospital after reading the few magazines lying around, each one with styles from days long past. They were picture book museums of fads that never quite caught on and weren't going to any time soon. Waiting in a sterile white room with nothing to do was the epitome of awkward. Of course, lately everything was. It was hard to talk or think. It all went back to the ugly disease that had stolen their lives. It was in the driver's seat, choosing everything from how fast they went to which direction they turned. They were nothing more than passengers expected to pay the fare when the journey was over.

"Is it still sore?" she asked, not wanting to count the tiles on the ceiling for the seventh time since they had been shown in.

Jason lifted his arm and rotated it from the shoulder. "Yeah. The pain is becoming regular now. I suppose it has something to do with..." His words faded.

"You should tell the doctor," Chris suggested.

Jason let out a soft chuckle. "What good would that do? They aren't doing anything for me as it is. Why add another problem to the list of unsolved?"

"Good afternoon. I'm Doctor Patel." The door closed behind a mid-aged woman.

She was like the slew of other medical staff they had met in the past month - each one as unremarkable as the other. Chris was sure to someone they were the reason the sun rose and set each day, but to her every new doctor or nurse was a white coat, a clipboard with illegible scratchings and the next person without any answers. She didn't remember their names and hardly recognized faces. The truth was, she didn't expect to see this woman more than twice... giving her the benefit of the doubt, she decided three times was the magic number.

"Doctor," Jason said, acknowledging her presence. Even in the worst of situations, his pedigree shone through.

"It's been a long road," the doctor said, taking a seat.

Chris wasn't sure why the woman's lack of eye contact sent shivers down her spine. She was used to people avoiding them. Cancer was a dirty word - one not used in the best social settings and worse than any swear she could think of. If she had her choice, it would have been eradicated from the English language.

"I have the test results in," the doctor continued. "I wish I had better news. The spots we found are a form of lung cancer."

Jason's hand rubbed over his eyes, sliding down to cover his open mouth before falling to his lap. "What's the next step - surgery?"

The doctor forced a meek smile that lasted less than a split-second. "I'm afraid we are past that option. The cancer has already moved into surrounding tissue and part of your rib bones. It is inoperable."

"There must be something we can do!" Chris exclaimed.

"We can set up radiation treatments," the doctor explained. "There will be prescriptions for the pain as well."

"I have a question," Jason stated. "When is a person considered cured of cancer? Is there a point where they can ever breathe easy again? A point where they can say they beat the beast?"

Doctor Patel's lips closed, curling slightly downwards, her head nodding. "A person is considered cured if they are free of all signs of cancer for more than five years."

"Five years?" Jason echoed. "That would start after treatments?"

"I need to explain, the treatments you will be receiving are palliative," the doctor stated. "They may extend your life, but are more to keep you comfortable. We can begin treatments Monday. I'll have the nurse print you out a schedule."

"Thank you, Doctor," Jason said, shaking her hand.

The tingling sensation running through Chris's body was new. Numbness had burrowed its way in and was taking up residence. It was her new normal; her future. Even the burning sensation of coming tears was missing, replaced by disbelief served with a side of shock. Her mouth formed a grim line - glossed over eyes, blank as unused notepaper. She was lost - her mind a maze of tangled cobwebs and movements robotic at best. She felt his hand touch hers.

"It's not that bad," Jason said, smiling.

Her lips parted but no words formed. A guilt washed over her soul. If she was in such a state over the news, she couldn't imagine what he was going through.

"Hey," Jason said, cupping her chin in one hand to force their gazes to meet. "It is going to be rough, but it's only five years."

Chris's eye's widened. "You did hear what the doctor said, right?"

"Yeah," Jason said. "Five years." The look in his eyes was reminiscent of a child on Christmas morning - alive, enthusiastic and more than a little excited.

There was more to be discussed, but she couldn't voice it. This was the first time in months he had held her hand. For the brief walk between the examination room and their car, they were a normal happy couple again. It was as if reality had been washed away and one of her own fantasies was left in its place. She savoured the moment, not wanting to lose even a fraction of a second. Gloom was hanging like the shadow of an incoming storm. She could smell its dampness in the air and feel the chill in her bones. As the car door closed, it sealed it in with them. There was no escaping the cold grip pressing on her chest. She was suffocating under the burden.

"Are you sure you heard her?" she asked, biting her lip in regret for every word. Was it fair to take away the unjustified joy he'd found?

"Yes," Jason replied. "It's a five-year recovery time." He took her hand again, this time bringing it to his lips and gently grazing the back with a kiss

The horn sounded from the weight of Chris's head hitting the steering wheel. She bolted upright. How was she supposed to choose? Did she leave him in denial? A part of her knew he needed to hear the truth - he needed to accept what was to be and make the most of the time he had left.

"It's a five-year recovery time for people who manage to rid themselves of cancer," Chris whispered. "Not everyone does that."

"What are you saying?" He asked, releasing his grip. "You don't think I can get better?"

Her hand fell like her emotions had when she heard the diagnosis. The anger mounting in his eyes became daggers, stabbing her repeatedly where it counted the most - her heart. Still, somewhere deep inside, they both knew it wasn't hers that would stop beating first.

"I want nothing more than for all this to go away," Chris cried. Tears fell freely, cascading down her cheeks and soaking the front of her shirt. It wasn't enough to wring out, but she could have passed for being caught in a short shower without an umbrella. "But I heard what the doctor said and I think we need to prepare for what could be."

"What is it you think the doctor said?" Jason asked, his gaze locked on the pavement outside the passenger window.

"You have stage four lung cancer," Chris started. "That means they can't remove it because it has already spread."

"And."

"And," Chris said, her words shaking. "They aren't offering you a way to get better. They are only trying to make the time you have as comfortable as possible."

"I see," Jason said. "In all this, did she mention how long I have left?"

Chris's neck snapped upright. "No," she said, shaking her head. "We didn't ask."

"We probably should have," Jason whispered.

"Yeah," Chris agreed. "We should have."

Chapter Fourteen

Until Jason's next appointment, the stupidity of not asking for a time frame plagued her. It was moments wasted worrying for no reason. As it turned out, there was no definite answer. Cancer was a fickle disease. Every case was unique. It could have been months or years. While a doctor could have given them an average time of a year maybe more, it was up to Jason's body. Strangely enough, people seldom actually died of the cancer - it just earned the credit. The most deadly serial killer in history was a fraud. More often, it was a secondary disease that actually did the killing.

They'd been to several treatments. She glanced over his growing pile of medications, picking out the morning doses. The main ones were pain pills. They unfortunately caused constipation and an upset stomach. Little clear yellow bottles appeared, each meant to cure the side effects from his other medicine. Then there was a topical cream to put on to treat the radiation burns; vitamins to keep his strength up; depression medication, anti-anxiety pills and a concoction she still had no idea what it was for. She hated each and every one of them. How had society come to this? Giving someone pills to cure what other pills did and treatments that hurt more than healed didn't make sense.

She placed a single flower in a vase on the tray. It was the same as every morning - a full breakfast with juice and coffee. He'd try to eat, but most would become worm food in the backyard composter. The signs of weight loss were starting to show - a thinning of his face and the beginnings of wrinkles appearing where muscle had once kept his body firm.

"Thank you," Jason said, offering a meek smile from behind the desk.

Setting up a workspace in the spare room was the first step in his acceptance of the cards fate had dealt him. Each day started with researching things for his bucket list, and as time went on, legal documents to get his affairs in order.

There had been another decision: lying in bed doing nothing was not the way he wanted to spend what precious time he had left. Up until then, he had been solely existing day-to-day, only leaving the house for appointments. A new agreement meant their date nights were back once a week. There was no sense in living if all he accomplished was merely avoiding death. Dinner out with his wife was a luxury he refused to give up. They needed it.

"Chris," Jason said. "There are some things I want to tell you."

"Like what?" Chris asked.

"I want you to know how much I love you," Jason started.

"I love you too," Chris replied. "I need to clean the bedroom..."

"Chris," Jason interrupted. "I need to go over everything so you know where to find the information you need when the time comes."

Chris froze. "Right now?" she asked, clearing her throat. "I have a tonne of things to do. We can go over that later."

"Chris," Jason whispered. "You told me I needed to accept things... now I'm telling you the same thing. We need to be prepared. I want you to be taken care of. I want you to know I love you."

"I do know you love me," Chris muttered, her sleeve becoming a tissue. "We have time still." She sniffled, inhaling deeply. "You can't get rid of me yet. Besides, look at you. It's not like the end is around the corner. You haven't even finished your treatments yet."

"How about I open a file on your computer? You can look at it when you are ready," Jason suggested.

Chris nodded, her lips sealed tight.

Jason looked down at the single flower in a small white vase and smiled. "A single flower," he said. "I've always been partial to petunias, the ones you plant out front every year."

"What?" Chris questioned.

"At my funeral," Jason explained. "All I want is one damn petunia, preferably cut from our garden... nothing more."

"Now you are being silly," Chris blurted out.

"I'm serious," Jason said.

"It's good to see you smile," Chris mumbled. "It's been a while."

She remained still, watching him stand. His arms extended around her waist, drawing her close. The beating of his heart consumed her. It was the same as it had always been - strong and steady. Her eyes closed, savouring the rhythm of his breath. This was how things were supposed to be. For a moment a part of her forgot everything that had happened, but that was short-lived. His icy touch cupping her chin reminded her all was not okay, still she gave in to the soft kisses his lips gave to hers - a moment worth treasuring for eternity.

Chapter Fifteen

The bubbles had already faded by the time Chris finished the last of the dishes. She watched the water swirl down the drain. There was no need to dry them, they were headed for the dishwasher. It had become a ritual for her since Jason fell ill. Washing everything twice and disinfecting as well as cleaning was a necessary part of life now. Even so much as a cold could land her husband in the hospital.

She chuckled at the arrival of a low whining noise. That meant it was feeding time. They say animals know when their owner is sick. Chris could attest to that. The past week, Miracle had barely left Jason's side.

Stuck in a trance, she watched her furry friend devour kibble from a silver bowl by the door. The last crumb had no chance of evading the pink tongue that sought it out. Chris laughed as his legs tangled trying to scurry across the ceramic tiles and getting no further than if he had been on a treadmill. A little creature with determination. No matter what, he was making it back to Jason. But why? Even as a dog, he must have known he couldn't make his master better. Perhaps spending as much time together as possible was enough to comfort both of them.

A thump from upstairs sent shivers down her spine. Her legs moved without commands, taking two steps at a time all the way to the top. It was Miracle's bark that led her to the makeshift office. There was no time to think.

She staggered forward, barely feeling a jolt to her knees worthy of bruises. Her legs were nothing more than deadweight, hitting the ground beside Jason's lifeless body. There was no stopping the tears from falling. Instinctively, she watched his chest, hoping for a sign of life - none came.

"Jason!" Chris yelled, grabbing his shoulders. "Jason, can you hear me?"

She grasped his shoulders and shook. His arms flapped by his sides in motion with the force of the back-and-forth movement. Her mind swirled with no clear vision. There had been no manual for this. No doctor had prepared her for that moment. All sense of reasonable thought had forsaken her. "Jason!" She pounded on his chest.

"What," Jason whispered, sputtering a cough with his words. "How'd I get on the floor?" He pushed himself into a sitting position.

Chris threw her arms around him. "I thought I lost you. You stopped breathing. I didn't know what to do." She sniffled. Her weight rested against him, heart still threatening to explode from her chest. Not even a paper bag would have controlled her breathing, only time could.

"I'm okay," Jason offered. "My neck is a bit sore, though."

"Sorry," Chris replied. "I may have shook you."

Jason sighed. "Guess we know panic isn't your strong suit."

"Yeah," Chris admitted. "It's easy now to think of all the things I should have done. When I saw you, my mind went blank."

"It's okay," Jason said, rubbing her back. "Maybe we should make a list to help... in case it ever happens again."

"Calling for help should probably be at the top of the list," Chris admitted. "We need to take you to the hospital and find out what happened. Do you remember anything?"

"Nothing," Jason answered. "Last thing I remember was opening my email account. A cough took me by surprise. Then, I saw you. Are you okay?"

Chris chuckled. "You are asking if I'm okay. You're the one who wasn't breathing for at least a minute. I'm just the scatterbrain who couldn't keep it together."

"I'm serious," Jason said. "Look at you, you're shaking." He brushed the hair off his wife's forehead. "And clammy."

She blinked twice, trying to avoid another onslaught of tears that would soak both of their shirts.

Jason's face wore the signs of stress - fatigue engraved in every line. She traced them with a single finger. She hadn't noticed until that moment the signs of age that had crept in so quickly, sucking the years away from him - from them. *Damn cancer.*

"I'm sorry," she muttered.

"Don't be," Jason replied, grasping her hand. Soft kisses brought back the warmth that a moment ago had been lost.

"We should go to the hospital," Chris stated.

Jason nodded.

She flashed a weak smile. It was all she could manage to mask how she really felt - worried. Now, there was even more to make her feel that way. The simple task of going down the stairs had her on edge. Was he stable? What if he passed out halfway down? Could she catch him? Was she strong enough?

She held her breath until Jason was safely on the main floor. He exchanged a housecoat for a jacket, but kept the slippers. Shoes had been the first thing he gave up when the treatments started. Other than it being easier, she wasn't sure why. Perhaps they provided a sense of comfort; a sense of home. The door made a creaking noise behind them, but didn't close, only locking after two attempts.

"I need to get that fixed," Jason said, eyeing the door frame. "When I get home, I'll make some calls and take care of it."

Chapter Sixteen

Chris pressed the button again, knowing it wouldn't make the elevator come any faster. If it had been the first or second floor, she would have opted for the stairs, but the eleventh floor was a bit far to sprint. Tapping her foot, she pressed it again.

"In a hurry?" a white-haired lady asked.

"My husband is being discharged this morning," she replied, flashing a weak smile. "I don't want to keep him waiting." That was the best answer she had. There was no reason for her to be anxious. The doctors hadn't been able to find anything wrong. Still, there was a sense of urgency in that back of her mind she couldn't ignore.

Chris let out a sigh of relief when the familiar ding of the elevator sounded. She tapped her foot, waiting for others to load into the small lift, sighing at every hand that stopped the doors from closing so another person could join in the ride. Her eyes widened, watching each number light up as visitors and staff chose their floor of destination. Each stop felt like a lifetime. A rage was building inside her core that she knew she had no right to feel, and yet she couldn't control. If looks could kill, the daggers thrown from her gaze would have landed her in jail for multiple life sentences.

Chris' composure never had a chance to recover before the doors opened to Jason's floor. She cleared her throat and stepped over the threshold, planning a calm walk. Her body had other ideas. Moving almost robotically, her legs took over; first to a brisk walk and ending in a jog, passing open doors and faceless patients along the way.

The smell of disinfectant stronger than usual alerted her to cleaning carts making their way from one room to the next or perhaps from the well-dressed woman emptying the contents of a wall hand sanitizing station into her palms. Someone obviously forgot to tell her cancer wasn't contagious. Not that it would have mattered if they had. There was a certain stigma attached to the ill. Nobody wanted to be in their shoes and there were those who went through extremes to make sure they weren't. If they truly cared for those they visited, they would have done some research or at least made an effort to understand the disease.

There was something ominous about the closed door that brought her to a full stop. The dryness of her mouth didn't prevent her from trying to gulp back the lump forming in her throat. She clenched the collar of her jacket with one hand, the other shaking as it reached for the handle. Once inside, her worst nightmares became reality.

Chris rushed to Jason's side, her gaze taking in all the tubes and wires connected to his body. If they hadn't been there he might have been simply sleeping. A single touch of his hand took the strength from her knees. She fell back into a visitors chair. He was hot - burning up from the inside.

"I thought I saw you arrive," a nurse said from the door.

"What's happening?" Chris stuttered in no more than a whisper.

"I left a message," the nurse answered. "Your husband is unresponsive."

"Unresponsive," Chris repeated. "I don't understand. He was supposed to be coming home. I'm here to pick him up." Tears fell, forming a path to her chin before dropping off to a new-found freedom.

"I've called the doctor to let him know you arrived," the nurse stated. "He'll be in shortly to explain."

Chris nodded, glancing back at the nurse. She'd seen her before, but had no idea who she was. She did, however, know the woman wasn't going to give her any more information. There was nothing to do but wait for another nameless white coat to show up and explain.

She sniffled. Her hand brushed the hair from her husband's face. She barely recognized him behind the puffiness of his reddened skin. There was a raspy noise that accompanied every breath he took. She couldn't tell if it was the oxygen mask over his mouth or his body struggling to stay alive.

"I'm here," she said, taking his hand. Her lips planted a gentle kiss against it, the same has he had done to hers hundreds of times. She bit her upper lip, trying to hold back a tidal wave of emotions and failing. "I love you," she whispered.

A gurgling noise accompanied his breath. It was like nothing she had ever heard before. Bubbles appeared in the mask. Chris didn't have to be part of the medical staff to know that wasn't supposed to happen. She screamed for help. Jason's doctor and the nurse appeared at the door, silence their unseen companion.

"Is he..."

"Yes," the doctor replied.

Her mind swirled. Nothing made any sense. "Why are you standing there? Why aren't you doing something?"

"He left his final instructions not to be resuscitated," the doctor explained.

Her hands grasped her head, not willing to accept what was happening as reality. "I have power of attorney," Chris blurted out. "Bring him back."

"Get the cart!" the doctor shouted over exchanged glances.

"Code blue," sounded over the intercom.

A member of the staff guided Chris to a private room, although, she had no recollection of which one. She slumped into a chair. Time slowed to a crawl as she counted each tear that fell. An animal stuck in headlights - that was what she was. Hypnotized, yet still watching the car come closer. Every instinct in her body warned her of the oncoming danger, yet she couldn't move. Her brain screamed run. It was too late. There was no avoiding the collision.

The door opened.

"Did..."

The doctor held up his hand. 'We successfully revived him... I know this is hard, but I need you to listen very carefully. Nine minutes is a long time to be gone."

"He will never regain consciousness..."

"No," the doctor affirmed. "He is on life support."

"You want me to pull the plug," Chris whispered.

"I can't tell you want to do," the doctor answered. "You need to decide for yourself. I can tell you I don't think he wanted to be kept alive artificially."

"No, he didn't," Chris muttered. "If you disconnect him, how long will he last?"

"Minutes to a few hours at most," the doctor replied.

"What happened?" Chris asked. "I was supposed to be taking him home."

"Jason had an infection. We didn't notice it because it was inside the cancer," the doctor explained. "It exploded inside his lungs. There was nothing anyone could do."

Chris nodded. "Can I have a few minutes with him first?"

"Of course," the doctor answered.

Chris held the railing mounted to the wall. She often wondered what it was for, but now understood. Her legs shook with every step. There was an emptiness in the room she hadn't felt before. She moved to Jason's side and grasped his hand.

"I'm so sorry," Chris stuttered, amidst sobs. "I love you so much. I hope you know that." Her hands covered her face. She felt an arm around her shoulders and accepted a box of tissues held out before her. "Is he in pain?"

"No," the nurse answered.

"Can you make sure he stays that way until the end?"

"We will," the nurse replied.

"I can't stay to watch you die again," Chris mumbled. "I can't. I'm sorry. I'm not strong enough for that."

"Is there someone you can call?" the nurse asked.

"No," Chris admitted. "I'll be fine. You'll call when..."

"Of course."

Chris made her way down the hall. In the background, she heard a woman's voice on the phone.

"We have a cancellation spot available."

Jason was now the one who passed away. He was the cancellation that gave someone else a chance to fight to stay alive. Everything had come full circle.

******

Chris slammed the door - twice. The last hour was a complete blur, including the drive home. Her eyes stung from tears crying tears of their own. She fell to her knees. A wave of guilt washed over her, dragging her down. If her tears didn't drown her, it surely would. What had she done? How could she have been so self-centered?

Jason didn't want to be revived. It was her who wanted him back. She wasn't ready to let go. He'd tried to prepare her and she hadn't listened. Her own insecurities forced him to live longer in a hell she'd never understand, but knew he must have been going through. It was all her fault.

She was a monster. How could she live knowing what she'd done?

Jason led his life thinking of her. When it counted the most, she wasn't able to put her own feelings aside and care about him. That realization would haunt her for the rest of her life. There was no recovering from facing yourself in the mirror and seeing evil glaring back.

She fell backwards into a sitting position, cradling her face in her hands. Furry paws climbed on her lap. A tiny head nudged her hands, licking the salty residue of falling tears.

"Miracle," she whispered. "He's gone."

Her arms wrapped around Miracle's body. She rocked back and forth, not wanting to let go. He wiggled, not happy with the constraint of her hugs. Her grip relaxed, one hand brushing the fur from his eyes. His ears perked up. He growled, followed by a whimper. A wave of tremors overcame Miracle's small body.

"What's wrong, boy?" Chris asked, using her sleeve to wipe her nose. "I'm right here, baby." Her hand stroked his back.

The phone rang in the background. Jason was gone and this time he wasn't coming back. Miracle's tremors continued, with an occasional cry thrown in. He knew his master had left. Chris tucked a blanket around him, offering a false sense of security, enough to calm uneasy nerves.

"Please be okay," Chris whispered in her pet's ear. "I can't lose you too."

The phone rang a second time.

"Mrs. Granet?" a woman asked.

"Yes," Chris answered.

"Your husband noted he wanted to donate organs." There was a pause. "We have established we are able to harvest his eyes for transplants."

"Harvest?" Chris' voice shook. "He's been dead for less than ten minutes."

"I am sorry for your loss," the woman continued. "But for organs to be usable we need to move quickly."

"Fine," Chris answered.

"There are papers that need to be signed."

"I'm not at the hospital," Chris explained.

"I realize that, Mrs. Granet," the nurse replied. "If you could come..."

"I just got home," Chris complained. "My husband is dead. I am in no condition to drive." An anger began to build inside the pit of her stomach.

"Can we fax it?"

"I don't have a fax," Chris snapped. "Email it, let's just get this over with. Make sure it is everything you need because after I send it back, I want you to leave me alone. My email is in Jason's file." She clicked end.

Not enough people had worried about Jason when he was still alive, but they sure were eager to use him to save others now that he was dead.

Chapter Seventeen

Funerals. Whoever thought of them clearly had making money in mind. Chris ran her hand over the back of a plush chair. Just days ago, she had sat in one just like it as a man dressed in black tried to help her decide what Jason would have wanted. He spoke softly and acted as if he cared, but he was first and foremost a salesman. He had his job nailed down like the lid of a coffin.

If she picked something towards the lower end of the pricing, he used words to make her feel like she was selling her husband's life short. She had loved him, after all, so shouldn't she give him the best money could buy in death? After spending more than she could afford came the hard question.

"How many will we be expecting?"

Chris was still bitter about that question. How could anyone know the answer? This wasn't a wedding or a baby shower - it was a funeral. One didn't simply send out invitations and ask for replies. On top of that, Jason's sickness had seen them both pull away from society. With neither of them having any family nearby worth mentioning, that left those few who happened to see the ad in the paper and showed up, plus a couple of standard funeral crashers who came for the food.

In the end, she selected a maximum of fifty guests, which was probably too many. It was the assurances of the funeral director that it was a standard number that clinched the deal. He even threw in the addition of a nice picture of Jason in the obituary - a tactic she once believed reserved for middle of the night infomercials. The cringe worthy words, *But wait! Act now and we'll throw in,* still ran through her mind when she thought about it.

That same photograph now sat on a table beside Jason's coffin. She placed the white vase, containing a single petunia from their garden, beside it. There were no other bouquets or arrangements allowed. Messing up his wishes had been a mistake she had made once before. That wasn't about to happen again.

Her eyes glanced at her wrist. A single finger tapped on the glass dial. It was early still. A fear of time passing too slowly forced her gaze to return. The opposite was true. Time was passing alarmingly fast and a few faces were appearing.

She smiled at Jason's personal assistant, mingling with a group of his colleagues. Her husband had never mentioned any of their names. They were most likely the unlucky ones chosen by the firm to attend. Appearance in advertising was everything.

In one corner stood an unfamiliar couple. They hadn't offered their condolences and scurried off to the reception area only moments after arriving. Chris thought about calling them out, but if they were that desperate for a sandwich and coffee, there was bound to be plenty left.

She had, after all, agreed to food for fifty - a number that wasn't going to be achieved.

Having only half those expected attend was a blessing in disguise. People at funerals seemed to lose their ability to socialize. She weathered the horrible questions: "How are you?" and "Are you okay?" Did they even need to ask? Her husband was dead. Of course she wasn't okay. Then there were the ones who wanted to take a trip down memory lane, not one of them realizing how painful their words were. Chris held her breath through each story, trying to avoid a makeup disaster - black mascara running down a face was the worst.

The few people she had wanted to see remained absent. It didn't matter how many times she surveyed the room, those she considered her closest friends never appeared. Her bottom lip quivered. She was truly alone. A moment of self-pity brought about the stream of tears she'd so desperately tried to hide. A tissue box appeared before her. She glanced up at the face of a stranger - one she knew better than anyone else who had attended.

"Thank you," Chris whispered. "You're Jon, right... our neighbour?"

"Yeah," he answered, shoving his hands in his pockets. "I saw Jason's picture in the paper and I wanted to pay my respects."

"Thank you," Chris repeated.

"I'm sorry," Jon said. "I know it doesn't help and there isn't anything I can say that could..."

Chris let out a faint chuckle. "Just please don't ask me if I'm okay."

"I wasn't going to," Jon admitted. "I mean, I get it."

"Right," Chris nodded. "Jason mentioned your wife was ill."

"She is," Jon affirmed. "I saw you set up a donation fund to the Cancer Society. I take it that means..."

"Cancer," Chris cut in. "Jason died of lung cancer."

"That night," Jon said. "I had no idea he was sick. I feel horrible for going on about my wife's situation when he was going through the same thing."

"Don't be," Chris replied. "We didn't find out until later that week. He had a fast-growing cancer, but it was an infection that actually killed him."

"You're lucky," Jon said.

Her gaze darted to face his, void of all expression.

"Oh, I didn't mean it like that," Jon said, beads of sweat forming on his brow. "I meant that you don't have to watch him suffer. My wife has been sick for some time. Now, every day I visit a little more of her disappears. Soon all that will be left is a shell of the person I loved and the cancer. It's like watching her die day after day and then knowing I have to do it all over again."

"That sounds horrible," Chris replied. "I guess in comparison Jason was lucky. He didn't even have time to finish the treatments."

"I should," Jon started, glancing around, "go." He pressed his lips together, his eyebrows raising and falling with widened eyes.

"Thank you for coming," Chris said.

She watched him walk out the open french doors, turn the wrong way and pass by again when he figured it out. Out of all the people, it was his presence that had the greatest effect on her. They shared a common bond - a terrible one, but common nonetheless.

Chapter Eighteen

Chris plopped down on the couch - the same couch as every other night. Miracle jumped beside her and after his usual full circle, he found the most comfortable position. His head rested on her thigh. Her hand instinctively ran through the fur on his head, her eyes never leaving the television screen. Tonight it was black and silent, as was the rest of the house. The phone no longer rang. There was nothing and no one left to avoid. She'd managed to alienate them all.

It wasn't that she didn't want friends. They simply didn't understand how it felt. It was difficult to hear the words, "Will your husband be joining you?" It was even harder to answer with, "My husband passed away." She'd even turned down an invitation to a wedding that listed her plus a guest. Her husband was dead. She had no one to bring.

That was about the same time pity ran out. The very thing she had been waiting for. No more "poor girl," or "I feel so bad for her." Unfortunately, the whispers had taken a turn for the worst. New painful words were uttered and no one cared if she heard them.

"She needs to just get over it."

"It's not like they were married that long. It was only five years."

"I lost my 'insert random name here' a month ago. You don't see me harping over it. People die, it's the natural order of things."

The converter struck the wall, batteries and plastic scattering on the ground. Cancer wasn't part of the natural order of things. She'd lost family members before: grandparents; parents. Their deaths left scars, but it was nothing compared to losing her partner; her other half.

She never realized how much he did for her; how much she relied on him. Every day that passed, she found something new she didn't know how to do or something she didn't know needed doing. Today it was the alarm system. Every door had a trigger that beeped when it opened. The back door started randomly going off at different times. She had no idea why.

"Do you know why?" Chris asked, staring at her dog. He'd become her shoulder to cry on, her best friend, her confident. Night after night, they watched shows and movies, discussing the plots and occasionally the news. She'd learnt what his different grunts and groans meant, or at least what she thought they meant. This time, however, he didn't seem to have any answers at all.

She sighed and pushed Miracle from her lap. "Looks like I have to do some investigating," she said. "You want to stay here?"

Miracle's ears perked up then flopped back down. He'd found a pillow just as comfy as her leg. It wasn't like she was going far anyways. She never did anymore.

Her desk hadn't been touched since Jason first found out about his sickness. There wasn't time or motivation to write. Her fingers stroked the keyboard, the familiar feeling sending shivers down her spine. She brought up a blank page: white; cold; empty - exactly how she felt. How ironic a writer relating to an empty file - an unwritten story.

She closed the page, straining her burning eyes to see the desktop background. The mouse's arrow pointed at a file, then another, searching for one that might have instruction manuals. It froze on the folder labelled Jason's file. She'd forgotten he made a file for all the things she might need to know. She wiped her face of a cold sweat and inhaled deeply. A double click and it opened. There was only one document.

My dearest wife,

If you are reading this, I must already be gone. I'm glad to see you made it back behind your desk. This disease took a lot out of me, but it hurt me more to see what it took out of you. At the end of this letter you will find all the information I could think of that you might need in the future. Hopefully, I haven't forgotten anything.

I wanted to tell you some of this in person, but you weren't ready to hear the words. I need you to hear them now.

My story might be over, but you are ready to start a new chapter. Put aside the sadness and live. I want you to write again. I want you to be the woman I fell in love with who saw the possibilities in everything.

I've been thinking about it lately and I've decided, life is like a toy. Miracles are the batteries that keep it running.

Everyone knows batteries aren't included. You have to go out and find them. Sometimes you even need more. A toy without batteries does nothing. It has no purpose. It simply exists. Life without miracles is the same.

I found you, my miracle.

I'm glad you found that little dog. I hope he has brought you some comfort. He is your miracle. That doesn't mean he has to be the only one. Keep your eyes open; seize the opportunities that appear; find another miracle. You deserve to be happy. That is my final wish.

I love you always

Jason.

Chris continued to read the lists of passwords and bits of information that had been left for her to make heads or tails of should a variety of different situations occur. Her finger slid off the computer mouse as she reached the end. Her head sat perched slightly tilted, staring at the screen. At that moment there was nothing. Her face was as blank as newly poured asphalt, every moment hardening it further until indifference was fully solidified in place. She blinked twice. The door alarm sounded again.

Her hand disappeared inside the top drawer. After fumbling around, it re-emerged, a screwdriver within its grasp. She stood, making her way to the back door. Her gaze examined every line, every corner, but came up empty. The front door perhaps held some answers. Fingertips ran across the top of the door frame and down the sides, finding nothing but dust she hadn't bothered to clean away. Even open, the door seemed to hold no answers. She slammed it closed. It popped open again.

Stretching her neck, she slammed it a second time, with the same result.

Her grip on the screwdriver tightened - knuckles turning white in the process. Her palms suffered, indented in spots where fingernails dug in. Her face distorted with disdain. Everyone has a breaking point. Chris had just found hers. In one swift motion her fist released, its contents sent hurling across the room. In the background the sound of shattering glass and Miracle whimpering from the adjacent room combined. Legs buckling, she fell to the ground screaming.

"Damn you!" she cried. "You said you'd take care of the door. You said you'd get it fixed. Why didn't you get it fixed? I don't know what to do!"

He left her alone; all alone, without a clue how to survive on her own. It wasn't fair. She breathed deeply, but the rage boiling within her refused to settle. There were no tears; no sadness. This was pure anger and hate. She hated that he was gone while she lingered on. As horrible as it sounded, she hated that he didn't fight harder and live longer.

She felt the energy drain from her body - exhaustion grabbing a hold of her and refusing to let go. The release of so many emotions in one day was too much to bear. This wasn't a normal go-to-bed-at-night tired. She was weary in mind and soul - dying slowly on the inside.

The basement hadn't seen a visitor since Jason passed away. She headed down, plopping back in his favourite chair. It reclined to a comfortable position. It wasn't long before Miracle joined her. He whimpered at the blank slate that masked her face, but put his head down nonetheless.

She could feel the muscles in her limbs weighing heavy, her eyelids joining in. There was no struggle to be had. Sleep took her within moments.

Chapter Nineteen

For a fleeting moment, Chris believed she was still asleep, lost in a fantasy land. Jon called her name, his face visualized in her mind. Was he her dream-man?

"Chris?" Jon called out.

Her tongue darted out, wetting dry lips. Her eyes snapped open. Within seconds she was on her feet. It was no dream.

"I'll be right up," she called out, her mind racing. What was he doing there? Why was he in her house? Memories of days long ago resurfaced along with two words: killer and psycho. She shook her head. Her days of being ridiculous were over.

As if reading her mind, Jon called out again, "I'm sorry for barging in like this, but your dog got out."

Her step quickened to the top of the staircase. Her gaze alternated between the small animal in Jon's arms and the broken door.

"I swear I didn't break it," Jon blurted out. "This little guy was chasing a butterfly. I thought you'd want me to bring him home."

"Thank you for bringing him back. I know you didn't break the door," Chris said. From his posture and tone she knew the face she was making. Jason often commented she had the ability to make him feel like he was making water turn into gold. "It's been broken for a while. Jason meant to get it fixed, but never got around to it. I haven't had a chance to..."

"I'm pretty handy with wood," Jon said. "Let me grab my tools and a few supplies. It won't take long and then neither of us have to worry about him getting loose again."

"Are you sure it's no trouble?"

"Yeah," Jon answered, flashing a dashing smile. He flipped the bangs off his face. "I can fix this. I'm happy to help."

"Thank you," Chris replied, taking her dog from his arms. "And you, little fella, what's this about chasing butterflies, huh?"

Miracle barked.

A low chuckle struck a chord within her, sounding an alarm to wake dormant emotions. Jon's laugh was warm and inviting and something she hadn't heard in a long time. She plopped down in the closest chair, holding Miracle in a hug. Her lips parted no more than a hair, curling up at the edges. A tingling sensation flowed through her fingers, toes and even her nose. A part of her she believed lost was waking. Emotions were stirring.

Miracle jumped from her arms, eager for release. In the best way a dog could, he welcomed Jon's return, tail and butt wagging as one.

"I wasn't gone that long," Jon said, smiling.

"He likes you," Chris explained. "You could leave the room and come back five minutes later and get the big I missed you dance."

"That's nice," Jon said, starting to work on the door. "I've thought about getting a dog, but never have. Seems like it would be good to have someone around that listens and loves unconditionally."

"Yeah," Chris replied, running her hand through her hair. "He's been my saving grace through all that's happened. I don't know where I'd be without him."

"Don't forget you need people too," Jon suggested.

"Um," Chris said, her voice lingering on the M. "Not so much. I still can't handle having to explain my husband is dead. It makes things awkward."

Jon alternated his gaze between her and the door frame without saying a word. His hands ran over the wood. He had a connection to it, knowing where to press or push to make it fit just right. Strong fingers caressed the grains, his eyes appreciating the lines and grooves. For a moment, she wished she was a piece of wood.

"I find people are always asking if someone will be joining me," Chris continued, shaking the previous thoughts from her head. "Like this." She held up an envelope that had been collecting dust on her desk.

"An unopened envelope?" Jon asked.

"Not just an unopened envelope," Chris explained. "It's a wedding invitation. My second since Jason's death. I know exactly what it says. Please RSVP with the name of the guest you will be attending with." Her cheeks puffed out, air taking its time to escape through closed lips.

"Okay," Jon replied, his attention on the door frame - attention she wanted.

"Obviously, I don't have anyone to go with - my husband is dead," Chris said, pacing. "I figure I can either not go, or spend the night having to explain to everyone I meet. Death and cancer aren't exactly uplifting topics."

"So, you chose not to go," Jon stated.

"I'd rather not be pity girl sitting in the corner alone," Chris said, crossing her arms. A pout formed on her lips.

"All done," Jon said, smiling.

"So fast," Chris commented, rounding her desk. She reached in the drawer, pulling out a cheque book. Her teeth clamped down on the inside of her cheek. Cash would have been better.

"Yeah," Jon said. "I told you it was easy."

"I know," Chris replied. "It's just... Jason put it off for so long. I figured it was a big job. I mean, I'm glad it wasn't."

"Yeah," Jon answered, wiping his hands on the back of his jeans, his tool box already neatly packed and ready to go. "I should take off."

"How much do I owe you?" Chris blurted out, waving the cheque book.

"Nothing," Jon replied. The corner of his lips curled up, but only on one side. A playful fire danced in his eyes mocking her. No one used cheques anymore. "Consider it a neighbourly favour."

"I have to give you something," Chris said. "At least let me make you dinner. Don't make me feel like a charity case."

"I'm," Jon stuttered, "busy tonight."

Chris bit her top lip. "Okay," she muttered. "Maybe another time." She flashed a weak smile and collected Miracle from his feet.

"Yeah," Jon answered, his head hung down. Less than two steps away it snapped back. "I'm free tomorrow night."

Chris's eyes lit up. "Tomorrow night is perfect. I'll see you then."

Chapter Twenty

"Hi," Chris said, opening the door.

"Hi," Jon echoed back. "It smells good."

Chris stepped to the side to allow her guest to enter. He'd cleaned up - not quite as fancy as at the funeral, but he'd made an attempt at looking presentable. The stubble that had shadowed his face the day before was gone and not a stain or rip was to be found in his attire. Her eyes lingered over the tight short-sleeved shirt that left little to the imagination. This man had muscles and not the buff from the gym type. They screamed of years of hard work.

"Hey, fella," he said, crouching down to rub Miracle's face.

Chris looked away, feeling a flush rising in her cheeks. "I hope you like lasagne. It's one of my specialities."

"I love it," Jon admitted. "I'd be happy with anything. It's been a while since I've had a home-cooked meal. My cooking is rather limited to barbeque and heating up the contents of a tin." He flashed an awkward grin.

Chris returned the same smile. How couldn't it be awkward? They were strangers, brought together by tragedy. The only thing they had in common was a spouse that had cancer and hers was dead.

"It's ready," she said, motioning for him to take a seat at the table.

"So, um," Jon started, "are you Italian?"

"No," Chris admitted. "Be careful. The dish is hot."

She'd argued with herself about how to serve dinner and, in the end, decided the best way to make the pasta towers was in individual oven-safe dishes. A true lasagne chef knew that the odds of it staying in a well-formed stack while still hot weren't very good. She wasn't about to serve a cold meal. The only other option was to present a messy plate of food. That was rather like burping in front of someone - one had to feel comfortable enough within the relationship before that could happen. They weren't at that stage... yet.

"It looks wonderful," Jon said, fidgeting with the paper napkin. He placed it on his lap, then moved it back to the table.

Silence was the enemy when people new to each other spent time alone. It sought out and destroyed any hope of friendships forming, leaving them with an awful taste in their mouths. At least with the dinner she made, the only flavour lingering in either of their mouths was garlic.

Unfortunately, silence had another plan up its sleeve. Chewing was amplified with no other noises in the background. It didn't matter what the food was. A part of her wanted to race to the other room and put some music on as a distraction, but it was too late. That was a mistake she'd never make again. For the time being, they had to take turns nodding and smiling between mouthfuls of pasta. Jaws moved slowly, trying to avoid smacking noises or worse churning.

The door alarm chimed. Chris let out a chuckle. Jon didn't have to tell her they were thinking the same thing - saved by the bell.

"Door alarm?" he asked.

"Yeah," Chris answered. "Apparently, I need new batteries. I just don't know what size or where to put them."

"They are watch batteries," Jon explained. "I can you show you where they go."

"It's probably somewhere easy to find, isn't it?" Chris grimaced. Pathetic wasn't a word she ever expected to be used to define herself.

"Yeah," Jon said, laughing. "It is - once you know where to look." He led the way to the back door and pointed to the inside frame at the top.

"Huh," Chris grunted, mouth open. It was hard to believe she missed it at all. She'd traced the outside of the frame, but not the inside. The white of the box blended in naturally with the colour of the trim.

"Got a screwdriver and watch batteries?" Jon asked.

"Yeah," Chris answered. She pulled open a drawer. "I always called this my everything drawer. If you need it and can't find it, it's probably in here."

"Every house has one," Jon said, rummaging through for the pieces he needed. "The most useful drawer in any home."

"Thank you again," Chris said. "For coming to my aid."

"Always a pleasure to help a damsel in distress," Jon said, adding a wink to the end of his words. "I have an idea. Why don't you make a list of all the little things you need help with? Once a week I'll come over, knock off a few and you can make me another delicious home-cooked meal."

"Are you serious?" Chris asked.

"We don't have to if you don't think it's a good idea..."

"No," Chris interrupted. "I think it's a great idea." She chuckled. "That would be amazing. You have to tell me what foods you like, though. I can make just about anything."

"Deal," Jon replied, starting the process of silencing the warning chimes.

Intentional or not, his muscles flexed with each turn of the screwdriver. The sleeve of his shirt, moved up his arm revealing the bottom of a tattoo. She summoned her self-restraint. Asking someone to take off their shirt on a first... her thoughts stuttered. This definitely wasn't a date. Walking away was the only choice. Watching from a distance was a more acceptable solution.

*****

Chris sat looking at her reflection in the mirror. The past month had seen her transform on one day every week. It had been subtle at first, a little bit of mascara and lipstick, then a curl or two in her hair. Today, she'd laid out a pretty dress. Hairspray sizzled as she wrapped the ends of her hair around a hot curling iron and held it in place.

"What?" she said, her head tilted toward Miracle on the floor.

He offered a low-pitched whine as a response, his paws covering his eyes.

"I can dress up once in a while," she commented. "It's not like I'm flirting or anything. There isn't anything going on."

Miracle offered another whine.

"Don't give me that," Chris snapped. "I have nothing to feel guilty about. We are just neighbours being... neighbourly."

Miracle barked, leaping down the stairs to the door.

She glanced at her image in the mirror. "What do you know?" Her gaze fell to the picture beside her hair brush - a wedding photo. Bottom lip trembling, she ran her fingers over Jason's image. "I'm not cheating. We agreed - as adults, we are capable of appreciating the beauty of the human form... look don't touch." She glanced at herself and then the picture again. It fell face down, followed by a frustrated sigh. Releasing the final curl, she pursued Miracle, a faint knock at the door catching her attention.

"I think you can add the doorbell to the list," Jon said.

"Great," Chris replied. "Looks like I'll need you for another week." The list had been getting shorter and she wasn't sure how many more jobs she could come up with. He'd taken on yard work already. Their evenings had also become longer as silence began to lose the war.

"I know that smell," Jon said, his grin reaching capacity. "You made my favourite." His eyes widened, gaze reaching the table. "And an apple pie too. It's my lucky night."

Chris listened intently to the details of Jon's day at work, never flinching or blinking until he was done. She'd come to appreciate having another person around: someone to lean on; someone to talk to. He didn't mention cancer, death or Jason. He also didn't talk about his wife. Loneliness was nothing more than snow in the spring thaw - melting away to warmer times. It felt good to let a little sun in to brighten the shadows she'd been living in.

Conversation was probably the most important thing people learnt growing up. Being able to communicate properly was as vital to a human as food, water or shelter. It was the basis for understanding, trust, friendship and love. If even just a smidgen off, it could also lead to misunderstandings, arguments and hurt feelings.

After dinner, Jon didn't run for the door anymore. He'd taken to sticking around and offering to help clean up, an offer she wasn't about to turn down. Still, the evening came to an end quicker than she wanted and they were saying goodbye for another week.

"Thank you," Jon said, "again."

"No," Chris replied. "Thank you. I don't know what I'd do without you. You've literally saved my life."

The space between them grew thick, silence making its final play. Words had forsaken them. She searched his eyes for an answer as to his lingering and found her own desire. She was tired of being alone. She wanted to feel loved and cared for. She wanted to be taken care of. Reflexes took over. She pressed her lips to his, offering him a solution to both of their needs.

"I'm sorry," Chris said, backing away from the gentle kiss she'd gifted. There had been no reciprocation on his part.

"No." Jon said. He gulped back, the lump in his throat that was making no effort to hide. "I'm sorry. I can't." His eyes watered. "I'm not ready. You're not ready."

"I know," Chris muttered, fighting back tears. "I shouldn't have done that. Please, forgive me."

"I have to go," Jon said. His pace quickened down the walkway.

"Jon," Chris called out. "Please don't go. I'm sorry."

He stopped for a split second, then continued on without looking back.

"Please," Chris cried, sliding to the ground against the closed door. "Please don't leave me. You're the only friend I have."

Miracle jumped into her lap to lick away the salty water drenching her face.

"What have I done?" Chris asked.

Miracle whined.

Chapter Twenty-One

Chris lifted her spoon and let the soup fall off in globs, back into the bowl from whence it came. She repeated the motion, splashing drops onto her housecoat. There was no reason to change during the day anymore. She had nowhere to go and no one to see. She pushed the bowl away, her appetite playing hide and seek, except she didn't feel like seeking.

A thud outside the front window told her the newspaper had arrived for the day. Instead of being placed neatly on the porch outside the door, once a week, it hit just below the window pane, winding up in the front garden. The only time the delivery boy seemed to find the porch was while collecting payment.

She sighed. The world could have another glimpse at her flannel pyjamas, terry cloth housecoat and fuzzy slippers. It's not like she was going to see anyone. There had been no sign of Jon since the incident weeks ago. She'd messed things up beyond repair.

You made your bed, now you are going to have to lie in it. She laughed at herself. It was a silly saying and she hadn't actually made her bed in over a week.

She squinted, the brightness of the sun's rays blurring her vision. She didn't have to see to know where to go for the missing paper. She tossed it in the air like a coin flip, barely catching it again before a car door slammed behind her. She spun around, hopes high that she might have another chance to apologize.

Her hands fell with her anticipation. It was only a middle-aged woman dressed in a blue suit. Chris watched her trudge across Jon's snow-covered lawn. The head of a hammer rose and fell against metal spikes. The house was for sale.

"Excuse me," Chris called out.

The woman eyed her up and down a few times before smiling. "Yes."

"The owner," she stuttered, realizing she had no idea what to say. "Did he decide to sell?"

"Yes," the woman said, rolling her eyes.

"Of course he did," Chris mumbled. "That's why you are putting up a sign. I mean... why did he decide to sell?"

The woman looked up from her sign. "I'm not sure I can answer that. I suppose there are a lot of factors. One of them being the market right now. It's hot! Spring is around the corner. Now is a good time to list."

"Really?" Chris replied, deep thought plastered to her face.

"Are you and your husband thinking about selling?"

Chris smiled. "It's just me," she answered. "And my dog. I hadn't thought about it. Maybe in the future, though."

"Here's my card," the realtor offered. "If you decide to sell, give me a call."

"Thank you," Chris said. Her attention focused on the card as she made her way to the front door. Glancing back over her shoulder, she realized she'd made a giant leap, even if it was technically a baby step. A smile graced her lips. The door closed behind her. but a new life was just beginning.

The newspaper landed on her desk, where it remained untouched. Chris swivelled around in her chair, her teeth clamped down on the end of a pen, waiting for the computer to boot up.

Her writing program opened to a blank page. It was the perfect place to start - a new beginning. This was a new Chris and it was going to start off that way with something she had never attempted before - a poem. A title appeared: *Time to Say Goodbye.*

One sad day your light faded away.
I brought you back in hopes you'd stay.
In selfish dreams I needed you there.
My whole world required your care.
By the time I realized it was too late.
You would now suffer to a new date.
I didn't worry about how you felt.
My mind clouded with the bad hand I'd been dealt.
To comfort me you tried to return.
I can only imagine the painful sting and burn.
Once again you put your needs on hold.

You always had a heart of gold.
If I could go back to that very night.
I'd let your soul fly peacefully into the light.
I am sorry I wasn't stronger.
I only wished you'd lived a little longer.

A smile crept over her lips. She wasn't a poet, but to her what she'd written was more beautiful than anything that came before it. A new file name, 'Me,' became its home.

"Don't worry," she whispered. "I'll be adding more to keep you company in the future. Sh, it'll be our little secret place."

Double-clicking on her writing file, the last novel she had worked on appeared on the screen. She didn't even need to read what had already been written. Her fingers danced across the keyboard, making their own clicking music. Black words graced the white of the screen. Everything flowed as it had so long ago. She didn't miss a beat. The only holes around were pot holes in the road outside. Her plot was sound and her writing, a work of art - even if it was a horror novel.

Miracle lay by her feet. His leg shook in his slumber. Chris smiled, knowing her pet was deep within his own fantasy realm of bones and fire hydrants, perhaps even a cute poodle would make an appearance. She saw the possibilities.

The heaviness in her eyelids disappeared along with that which had plagued her heart. Stories that had built up over time poured out. Her slender fingers moved faster than they ever had before. They were racing to the end of one thought so they could start another. The ideas, the tales, the characters, they all wanted out. They wanted to be told; to be heard.

A full day and thousands of words later, the effects of lack of sleep began to show. Although she couldn't silence the beast that had been woken, it would have to wait. A novel wasn't written in a day. Even if it was, there were re-drafts, edits, proofreads and formatting that had to happen before publishing. This book was special. It needed to be perfect. This book was her new beginning.

She picked up a picture of Jason, finally understanding what he meant. She loved him and that would never change. He'd always be a part of her, but she had more living to do and he simply wasn't there to be with her as she moved forward. Jon had basically told her the same thing.

It was time for her to learn to rely on herself. Once she did that, she'd be ready to let someone else in to share the future.

Chapter Twenty-Two

Chris cocked her head, trying to find the perfect angle to examine the doorbell. There was always a short break between writing novels. This one, she used to learn something new. After watching countless videos on the internet, she found her courage and bought the supplies she needed. Actually installing it was easier than she anticipated. There was a certain sense of accomplishment that went along with being able to fix something on her own. It was a long forgotten feeling, but one she wasn't planning on taking for granted in the future. She was a strong independent woman, capable of relying on herself.

The door closed easily. All that was left to do was try it out. She felt a lump in her throat. A cold sweat added a shimmer to her forehead, the pesky sort of shine supermodels carried powder with them for. Testing her handiwork was worse than getting the first review on one of her books. She sucked in air, filling her lungs to capacity and reached for the handle. Chimes rang before her hand had a chance to turn it.

"Hello."

"Hi," Chris answered. "Carrie, right? Come In. Thanks for stopping by." She'd completely forgot about the phone call she'd made to the realtor. A smile graced her lips, not for her guest, but because the doorbell worked.

"My pleasure. I prefer to meet people in-person. The phone can be a bit impersonal. I guess you are ready to make a change," Carrie said. "So tell me your plans."

"I was thinking about downsizing," Chris replied. "This place is a little big for just me and him." She motioned with her head to Miracle at their feet.

"I can see that," Carrie said. "Do you know what you are looking for?"

Chris took in a deep breath. "Smaller, maybe two bedrooms instead of four - a bungalow could work. I'd need a functional kitchen." Miracle barked. "Oh, and he'd like us to be closer to a dog park. Preferably within walking distance."

Carrie laughed. "Of course! That makes perfect sense. Have you thought about a townhouse or apartment?"

Lines formed on Chris's face, her teeth grinding. "I... don't think that's a good idea. A lot of places are not pet-friendly these days. If they are, they hold the power to decide to go pet-less in the future. I don't want to take that chance."

"I understand," Carrie stated. "Any preference to location?"

"I hadn't really thought about it," Chris admitted. "I can work from anywhere as long as there is a good internet connection."

"Great!" Carrie exclaimed. "That makes it much more interesting. There are some amazing properties to be had if location isn't an issue. I'll send my assistant around to measure the rooms. After that we can set up a time for my photographer to stop by."

"Perfect," Chris replied. "Before you go, I have a question. I know this is a little out of the ordinary, but I was hoping you could help me."

"If I can," Carrie answered. "What did you need?"

"You handled the sale of the house next door," Chris began. White teeth closed over top of her bottom lip.

"I did," Carrie replied. "Were you wondering what it went for?"

"No... not exactly." Chris rounded her desk. A manila envelope appeared from within an open drawer. "I never got his forwarding address..."

"I can't give you that information," Carrie interrupted.

"I know," Chris said. "I wouldn't expect you to. I know you have privacy rules to deal with. I was hoping, if he didn't move too far, that perhaps you could give this to him."

"You want me to deliver an envelope?" Carrie asked.

"Yeah," Chris replied.

"I don't know," Carrie said. "This is against company policies. I could get in a lot of trouble if there was something in there that perhaps shouldn't be."

"You can totally look inside. It's not sealed or anything," Chris blurted out. "It's a copy of my latest book and a thank you note. Jon really helped me through a hard time in my life and I wanted him to know how much I appreciate it."

Carrie nodded her head. She took a deep breath in, accepting the package. "Alright," she agreed after quickly glancing inside. "I'm not a go between, though. This is a one-time thing. If he wants to message you back, that is up to him."

"Thank you," Chris cheered. "I won't mention him again."

Chapter Twenty-Three

Jon picked up the stack of papers in front of him. Inputting them into his accounting program was the beginning of the end. Now, he was on to his bank's website to send final payments to each of them. Once that was done, the weight of the world could jump off his shoulders and onto some other poor soul trying to find their way through life.

The breath he'd been holding escaped slowly with every send button he clicked. It was finally over. All the bills that had stacked up since his wife had fallen sick were paid. Some of the medical bills had been covered, but not all. That wasn't the worst of it, though. The prescriptions were the real killers. Medicine, especially for cancer, was expensive.

If he hadn't been such a proud man, he might have started what he referred to as a pity page. A place where he could have begged for money from friends and family. The more teary-eyed a person made the story, the more impact it had. That translated into donations. There were some legitimate causes that he himself had donated to in the past and those who truly needed help. He, however, wasn't one of them. He had a good job and skills to increase his income on the side. Bottom line, he was capable and wasn't looking for handouts. He had been managing too, even with the crippling mortgages.

When his wife was moved to a hospice, everything came tumbling down. Those last couple of weeks, he'd remained by her side. She didn't deserve to be alone when the time came. When living from paycheck to paycheck, taking time off wasn't a good idea. On top of that were the unavoidable funeral costs and bereavement leave.

Jon needed that time and had no regrets about selling the house. It was too big for a single person. They'd both come from a big family and wanted the same. That house could comfortably allow for four or more children. Moving back in with his parents allowed him to clean up his finances. Now that was done, he could begin to build a future again.

He leaned back on two legs of the kitchen chair, staring at the pile of paid bills. A smile of relief graced his lips. He'd been drowning for so long, he'd forgotten what it felt like to breathe. Debt was a disease in its own right.

The final piece of his sandwich popped into his mouth. It wasn't anything fancy... ham and cheese. The pickles he'd put on the side still sat on the plate waiting for their turn to be devoured.

"Hello!"

Jon's arms grabbed the table in front of him, avoiding a total wipe out by a narrow margin. The front two legs of the chair slammed back down on the kitchen floor.

"Did I scare you?"

"Surprised is more like it," Jon answered. "What brings my wonderful sister around for a visit? I didn't expect to see you until Thanksgiving."

"This," she answered, tossing a manila envelope onto the table. "Your old neighbour asked me if I could forward it to you."

"My old neighbour?" He echoed, grabbing the envelope. He tipped the contents onto the table. His smile expanded. "It's from Chris. How'd she know you were my sister?"

"She didn't," Carrie answered. "I guess I gave her a card when I sold your place. She gave me a call because she's selling hers."

"She's selling?" Jon repeated.

"When I went in to see the place, she asked me if I knew a way to get that to you," Carrie explained, grabbing one of the pickles off the plate beside her brother. "She said she wanted to thank you for helping her through a hard time. What's that all about?"

"I'm sure you can put two and two together," Jon teased.

Carrie took another bite of the pickle, her eyes fixed on her brother.

Jon sighed. "She must have told you her husband died of cancer."

"Nope," Carrie replied. "She said she lived alone with her dog."

"Really?" Jon questioned. He shrugged his shoulders. "Well, he did. Having spouses with cancer was a common bond between us. I helped her out with some stuff around the house and vice versa."

"Helped her out, huh?" Carrie joked.

Jon laughed. "It wasn't like that."

"Sure it wasn't," Carrie said, rolling her eyes. "She's cute."

"I wasn't about to have an affair while my wife was still suffering from an incurable disease in the hospital," Jon barked. "She is cute, though. I feel bad for not finishing the list of repairs for her."

"Like what?" Carrie pried.

"Just little things," Jon answered. "Like the doorbell didn't work."

"It works now," Carrie stated. "Guess she found another way to get it fixed."

Jon grinned. "Yeah, I guess she did."

"Don't even think about it," Carrie blurted out, waving the remainder of the pickle in her brother's direction. "I told her I wasn't playing go between and I meant it. If you have something to tell her, you do it yourself." She popped the pickle into her mouth.

"I wasn't going to..."

"Good," Carrie mumbled, still chewing. "Keep it that way."

Chapter Twenty-Four

Chris raced up the stairs at the sound of the doorbell. It took a few minutes for her to weave a path through boxes and packing material. Moving wasn't an easy task. This was the first time she'd attempted it alone.

"Hi," she said, pulling the door open.

"You'll swallow a fly if you aren't careful," Jon teased.

Heat rushed to her cheeks as she managed to close her lips, only opening them again to attempt to string together a few words. Another, "Hi," was all she could voice.

"Hi," Jon replied.

"I... I," she stuttered, "wasn't expecting to see you."

"Surprise," Jon replied, raising his eyebrows and opening his arms. "Could we take a walk? I'm sure you have someone in there that would like to come along."

"Let me grab his leash," she said, returning a moment later with an eager dog ready for action. "What's all this about?" A cool breeze picked up her hair, blowing it back off her face. Fall was on its way but not quite there yet.

"Carrie gave me the envelope," Jon admitted. "I wanted to thank you and... ask do I really remind you of a deranged killer re-enacting urban legends? How did you even come up with that from looking at me?"

"It's not you," Chris explained. "The character's description is based off of you. The rest was from that time I saw you cleaning your garage. I imagined what you could be putting down the storm drain in the road."

"And alligators were your first thought?" Jon blurted out, chuckling.

"Maybe not first," Chris replied. "But in the top ten."

"I have to admit your description of me was spot-on." His arm flexed directly in her view, the ink that had tortured her thoughts peeked out to slap her in the face.

The heat rose in Chris' cheeks. She'd forgot about that lusty description she'd added to the story. A little eye candy never hurt book sales, but in real life it was deadly. Torture was the word that came to mind. "I should apologize for that night," Chris said, changing the subject. "I had no right to assume..."

"It's okay," Jon interrupted, intense passion revealed in his eyes.

"It wasn't. You disappeared right after," Chris said, gulping back the saliva pooling in her mouth, unable to decide if it was her own feelings she was seeing reflected back at her. "You never came back. I never wanted that to happen. You even moved..."

"The situation isn't quite that cut-and-dry," Jon suggested. "I'm partly to blame as well. I was planning to come and talk to you. Patti, my wife, took a turn for the worse. I was at the hospital and then the hospice."

Chris nodded her head. Words had done nothing for her when she first lost Jason and they weren't going to help Jon now. If he needed anything from her it was to listen. All that time she had thought the silence was unbearable between them. It wasn't awkward. It wasn't a lack of chemistry. It was the best thing that could have happened and exactly what she needed. He'd orchestrated it on purpose, for her. This moment was her turn to understand what he needed.

"The house was a financial move," Jon admitted. "I couldn't stay by her side and make payments on three mortgages, plus medical expenses. After that, there were funeral costs. I made the right choice selling when I did. It had nothing to do with you."

"Coincidence," Chris mumbled.

"Yeah," Jon said. "I wanted to come back and see you, but not until after I sorted out the mess I was in. Yesterday, I paid off the last of it and coincidentally my sister brought over your package. Call it fate or destiny, but it was the right time... like someone was directing traffic."

"Wait," Chris said, stopping. Miracle tugged on the leash. "Carrie is your sister?"

Jon laughed. "She didn't tell you?"

"No," Chris complained. Her gaze followed a butterfly fluttering behind Jon's head. After performing a dance it floated down to the sidewalk, landing just out of the leash's reach. A yip of a bark followed. The butterfly held its ground.

"Hey, buddy," Jon said. "That butterfly is back, huh?" His question was answered by another bark followed by a low-pitched growl.

"Miracle!" Chris yelled.

"His name is Miracle?" Jon asked, his forehead wrinkling from raised brows.

"Yeah," Chris replied. "How did you not know that?"

"Huh... I don't know. I guess it never came up." Jon shook his head. A chuckle escaped from his throat. "It's odd, though, that your dog and I have something in common."

"You lost me," Chris admitted.

"My last name is Miracle," Jon explained.

"You're another miracle," Chris muttered. "You know... I could use a second one in my life. A girl can never have too many miracles, after all."

"Is that an invitation?" Jon asked.

"Someone once told me if I found a miracle, I needed to reach out and grab it," Chris replied. "I'm taking that advice."

The butterfly took flight, passing in front of both of their faces, before disappearing in the park.

"Thank you," Chris whispered her thoughts on the wind.

"I take it that butterfly has a story behind it... more than the part I already know," Jon said, wrapping his arms around her waist. He pulled her in tight.

"Yeah," Chris replied, smiling. "One day, I'll tell you all about it. That is, if you plan on sticking around and you'll have us."

"Hm. Let me think about that," Jon said. He leaned in towards her, one hand cupping her chin. Their eyes exchanged knowing glances before closing.

A soft groan escaped from her throat at the touch of his lips against hers. Even the cool pre-fall breeze couldn't put a damper on the warm glow building inside her.

"Jon," she whispered.

He licked his lips, leaving a trace of moisture glistening in the sun. "Yes."

"Can I ask you something?"

"Anything," he answered.

"I really need to know what your tattoo is," Chris blurted out.

Jon laughed. "Flexing those muscles really did get to you, huh?" He pulled up his sleeve. "It's the tree of life."

"Is there a special meaning?" Chris asked. Her fingers traced the ink. It looked complete, yet unfinished at the same time. Carved on the trunk were symbols: a cancer ribbon and a dollar sign. At the base lay fallen branches.

"You should look it up," Jon said. "Decide for yourself."

Chris nodded. "Challenge accepted."

Chapter Twenty-Five

One year later...

"Hey," Chris said, following Miracle to the door. Her arms wrapped around Jon's neck. "I missed you." Her lips brushed over his. "What's with the bandage?"

Jon laughed. "You don't miss a thing, do you?"

"It's the writer in me," Chris replied. "So did you add something new?"

"Did you ever figure out the meaning?"

"Of your tattoo?" Chris asked. "I never looked it up, but I have a pretty good idea."

"Go ahead," Jon urged.

"The tree represents strength and endurance," Chris started. "Basically it's your life. I figure the branches are people of importance who came into your life. The ones fallen, are now gone. You engrave the hardships you've survived on the trunk. It's not complete yet, because your life isn't complete."

Jon chuckled. "You really do see the possibilities in everything."

Chris laughed. "I try. Now your turn."

Jon removed his shirt, revealing a bandage. "I've added a little more to the story."

"You going to show me?" Chris begged.

The bandage peeled off easily. She gasped. It was beautiful. A mist formed in the corners of the eyes, but didn't sting. These were different tears - happy ones.

"This," Jon said, pointing to a new branch, "is you." As if anticipating her desires, he continued, "It's still a bit tender, but you can touch it."

Her fingers were already there, running over the lush green leaves, a small butterfly perched on one. "You added our friend."

"Yup," Jon said. "After hearing that story, I thought Mr. Butterfly deserved to be included. And this is Miracle." He pointed to a smaller branch lower down on the tree.

Chris snorted a laugh. "Hear that, Miracle. You got your own branch. Just remember this tree isn't for you to take a whizz on."

It was Jon's turn to laugh. He replaced the bandage. "So do you approve?"

"I do," Chris replied. "I just wish you'd waited a few months."

"Oh yeah," Jon said, side-eyeing her. "Why's that? You planning on going somewhere?"

"No," Chris replied. "It might have saved you another trip, though."

"Was there something you thought I should add?" Jon questioned, his brows furrowed.

"Well," Chris said. "You might want to add a small branch leaving some room for it to grow." Chris's lips curled up slightly.

"Are you trying to tell me something?" Jon asked, pulling her close.

The excitement was too much. "We're having a baby," she blurted out.

"A baby?" he echoed. "Are you sure?"

"Yeah," Chris answered. "The doctor called with the results just before you came home."

Jon dropped to his knees, his hands still on her hips. He pressed his lips against her stomach. "I love you both," he whispered.

Miracle jumped at his arm.

"Don't worry, buddy," Jon said, using one hand to pet his head. "I love you too. We're just adding another Miracle in our lives."

"And the butterfly made another appearance," Chris said.

"I never thought of that." Jon said. "Another coincidence..."

"I think at this point, there's no way it's a coincidence," Chris answered. "I'd like to think someone's looking out for us. Who knows, maybe it's even loved ones making sure we find our way."

Jon shook his head. "I like that... our own guardian angels."

"They'll always be a permanent part of our lives," Chris said. "And now they are helping us move forward. It would make a good book, don't you think?"

Jon got to his feet. His lips met hers. "As long as there is a happily ever after."

A message from the Author...

Although this is a fictional story, grieving is a very real process. It is important to know that no two individuals will experience it in the same way and certainly not in the same amount of time. If you or someone you know are going through the grieving process, there are people who can help. Talk to a doctor, a religious figure, a teacher or a grievance counsellor.

There is **NO** medical advice in this book. Please seek proper medical care for grieving and depression.

I hope you enjoyed reading *Miracles Not Included* as much as I did writing it. Watch for new books coming soon.

Other Titles from C.A. King

Shattering the Effects of Time

Join the Shinning brothers, Jessie, Dezi and Pete as they set out on a quest to save their younger sister. No magic known to them or their friends has ever been able to reverse the grip of time. A few legends, however, exist mentioning ancient items that may hold the key to do exactly that.

This brand new series will take you on a search for the Fountain of Youth and Mermaids; a quest for the Holy Grail; a trip to visit Daryl the mountain guru, in the hunt for the Cinamani Stone; on a search for Ambrosia, the food of the Gods; and other adventures.

When Leaves Fall: A Different Point of View Story

Ralph wakes up to what others only experience in a nightmare. Chained to a shed, he has no idea where he is, or who his captor is. His memories a blurred at best. As the days press on he finds himself experiencing a roller coaster of feelings. Hunger, thirst and pain become his only companions. Flashbacks of a happier time are all he has to keep him going. As his situation deteriorates, he finds himself doubting the very things he wants most - a family.

When Leaves Fall is a dramatic-thriller with a twist. Keep the tissue box close for the ending.

Tomoiya's Story

A Vampire Tale. She had a secret but she wasn't the only one who had something to hide.

Book I ~ Escape to Darkness

Book II ~ Collection Tears

Book III~ Coming Soon

Peach Coloured Daisies: A Cursed by the Gods Story

He couldn't die. An ancient curse meant she always did. This time, that was going to change - one way or another.

When Daisy's grandmother, her last living relative, passes away, she doesn't know where to turn. Things go from bad to worse when a local psychic tells her about a curse. Alone and confused, she ends up in front of her college professor's office, ready to cry her heart out in his arms.

Matt Demi might be the son of a God, but he's living the life of a cursed man. He's had to watch the woman he loves die on her twenty-first birthday countless times. Nothing he does seems to be able to affect the outcome. When she shows up at his office scared out of her wits by a psychic's prediction, he vows this time will be different.

With only three days, Matt will need to embrace a side of him he swore off long ago to save her, but will he lose himself in the process?

Flower Shields: A Four Horsemen Novel

Meet the four horsemen: Michael, Gabrielle, Uriel and Raphael. For centuries their job has been to guard the gates of hell, making sure they never open. Without the keys, there was never any real threat. That's about to change. There are rumours on the horizon that demon followers unearthed scrolls that explain exactly how to find the lost keys. This new battle is a race to see which side locates them first.

Michael couldn't care less about the love story behind how and why the world was created. In fact, nothing matters to him other than keeping the gates to hell closed. If one of the lost keys ever fell into the wrong hands, all humanity would be doomed. He's not going to let that happen - at any cost.

****

Tara's life is nothing short of a disaster. She's managed to flunk out of college with about the same amount of dignity as every relationship she's been in. The only constant in her life has been her love for flowers. When she's attacked at work, a stranger comes to her aid. Michael might be good-looking, but he's also arrogant, bossy and crazy. He's also her only chance to figure out who attacked her and why. Should she follow her heart and trust him - or listen to her head and run?

The Portal Prophecies

These great titles in C.A. King's The Portal Prophecies series are available now at most online book retailers:

A Keeper's Destiny

A Halloween's Curse

Frost Bitten

Sleeping Sands

Deadly Perceptions

Finding Balance

The prophecies are the key to their survival. Can they solve them in time?

Surviving the Sins: Answering the Call

The prophecies are being rewritten. This time someone is using the seven deadly sins: Lust; Gluttony; Greed; Sloth; Wrath; Envy; and Pride, to unlock an ancient evil. The book falls into Jade's hands to answer destiny's call. Can she survive the sins?

Surviving the Sins: Pride

No one is safe when a witch's pride is at stake.

Prudance is back in Pewterclaw, and she isn't about to give up her prestigious status without a fight - especially not because of vampires. As an eighth-generation witch, she plans to do whatever it takes to stop the proposed new legislation from becoming law, including waking the dead for help.

Humility isn't in her vocabulary. With an ego spinning out of control and ancestral power at her fingertips, Prudance weaves a plot to keep Jade and Gavin separated. Will it be enough to satisfy the spirits she summoned?

When her pride costs more than she bargained for, someone has to pay the tab - but who will it be?

Surviving the Sins: Lust

What Mother doesn't know won't hurt her.

Lucinda has spent her entire existence running The Organization and looking after Mother's needs without complaint. That's about to change. A burning desire had manifested inside her - one she could no longer deny... Lust.

When Constable Safron Black shows up unexpected with news of an imprisoned God, Lucinda unravels. With power fuelling her passion, she'll do anything to make Morynx her mate.

*****

Jade and her friends find themselves at a standstill. They have already failed to stop Pride from completing its task and they haven't located any victims for the other six sins. A strange fire in the municipal office puts them hot on the trail of what could be answers. Will they be in time to stop the dial from moving and further opening the way for Morynx?

www.ingramcontent.com/pod-product-compliance
Lightning Source LLC
Chambersburg PA
CBHW020622250626
47154CB00004B/1630